and then it rained..

coz life ain't
always a fairytale

and then it rained...

coz life ain't
always a fairytale

Gaurav Dashputra

Srishti
PUBLISHERS & DISTRIBUTORS

SRISHTI PUBLISHERS & DISTRIBUTORS
N-16, C. R. Park
New Delhi 110 019
srishtipublishers@gmail.com

First published by Srishti Publishers & Distributors in 2012
Copyright © Gaurav Dashputra, 2012

All the characters and incidences described in this book are a work of pure fiction. Any resemblance to any person dead or alive is purely coincidental.

Typeset in AGaramond 12pt. by Suresh Kumar Sharma at Srishti

Dedicated to all the people I have hurt…
I think everyone who knows me has been hurt by
me one way or another.
It might have been intentional or not.
So this book is dedicated to EVERYONE

ACKNOWLEDGEMENT

Ever since I was a little boy I had always dreamed of delivering a speech like this in one of those top end Bollywood award functions like Filmfare and all. But since that looks like a farfetched possibility now...I guess I will make the best possible use of this space given to me.

Firstly I would like to thank Srishti Publishers for giving me the opportunity to work with their esteemed Publication house and for all their support.

I wanna thank God for giving me this life. I wanna thank my parents for all their love and support...Mom, Dad you have given me all that I ever asked for and much more...I love you.

I wanna thank my sis Divya for being such a sweetheart. Sis you are the grandmother I never wanted and yet I adore you from the bottom of my heart.

A big thanks to Vedashree Jathar for being not just my elder cousin but a friend, Kshitij Jathar for not just being the coolest brother but for giving me a place to crash whenever I went broke, Parvati Vaze for being the star sister I always dreamed of. I love you guys. Here I would also like to thank their respective boyfriends and girlfriends for not keeping them all occupied so that they had time for me ☺

I wanna thank all my friends from school and college for helping me shape my life the way it has. I wanna thank all their respective boyfriends and girlfriends too for tolerating me.

I wanna thank Purna Nangia because without her I would have never written this book in the first place. Thanks for being there for me always ☺

"Hey I wrote another chapter...you wanna hear it?" Is something

I would often ask Ritu Banerjee after calling her in the middle of the night. Ritu thank you so much for listening to me and giving in your valuable inputs towards the story. If it weren't for you…the book would have never been completed. And Thank you for being single too and sparing me from the horror of a possessive boyfriend's wrath.

I wanna thank Vartika and Himanshu Patil…for being ever so supportive of my work.

Thank you Kunal Singh and Mohit Vashista for being the worst best friends ever. *Dost ho toh in jaise ho varna na ho.* The guys never read even one page of what I wrote. But jokes aside…I love you guys…you complete me in the most un-gay sense possible. A big thanks to Sheena Ali for being the sweetest girl I know and for being my mother away from home.

I would like to thank all my childhood friends…Prateek Chakraborty, Jayant Daksha, Ajinkya Purohit, T.Z Mathew, Sidhant Kaushik, Pratyaksh Rawat, Rahul Chaubey. Without you guys school wouldn't have been a joy ride.

I would specially like to thank Abhilash Ruhela who also goes by the name of BoL_Blogger on twitter for all his help pre-publishing. Bro you write one of the best blogs in this country. And I highly recommend everyone to read it. Well another reason why I am including his name here is to butter him up so he writes a good review about my book on his blog. HaHaHa…but seriously bro you are fabulous.

I would like to really thank Mumbai and the people of Mumbai for being such a huge inspiration. And I also thank Nagpur and the people of Nagpur for all the love that they foster for me.

I would like to thank all my friends on Facebook for tolerating my zillion status updates. I love you all.

I would like to thank all the women in my life…My ex-girlfriends, my school friends, my college friends, the ones I had a crush on, the ones who had a crush on me, the one whom I loved, the one who got away, the most beautiful ones, the not-so-beautiful ones, the darn ugly ones…on second thought maybe I can skip the ugly ones. Thanks for being there and giving me a chance to understand your impossible species.

If I have forgotten any names it's mostly because I don't like them or I owe them some money.

And lastly but most importantly I wanna thank Mr.Shah Rukh Khan for being my biggest inspiration. Sir if you ever read this…I would like to tell you that everytime I see you on screen…in a movie or on TV…You make me believe that life is indeed beautiful.

— Gaurav Dashputra

JUST A WORD OR TWO

There comes a time in everyone's life that they think why did life have to be the way it is? Why can't it be more predictable? Why can't the world go on the way they want it? Why is it that every time you think you have found the love of your life the world comes crashing down on you? Many of these questions we either find answers to or we just pass them off as a phase. Whatever it is there always are those gloomy days we just have to live by. But then as the mighty Achilles said "gods envy us because we are mortal, because any moment may be our last, that you'll never be here again you'll never be as beautiful as you are today" so I believe we should live by it and enjoy every moment because after every hot summer it rains....

PROLOGUE

I sat on the cliff where it had all begun and looked at the lake in front of me. The water had the same greenish tint. I wondered how my life had changed so drastically in the past three years. Did I have any regrets? Maybe a few. A dream left unfulfilled. A few words left unsaid. A relationship which never ran its due course. A friendship left in shambles. An untimely death. Was all this worth the pain?

Today as I sat on this cliff with the summer of my life at its peak…I didn't need the answers of those million questions my heart asked me. I didn't need anyone to tell me that it was all going to be okay. I did not want a breeze of happiness to blow through my life. All I needed was peace. All I needed was the rain after scorching summer.

I wanted the heavens to shower upon me and lay my misery at rest. Today as I sat on this cliff…my entire life flashed in front of me. I had come to the end of my journey. It had its own ups and downs but what a hell of a journey it was. Only if this road didn't pass through a town of broken hearts, things would have been so wonderful. But I think that is how life is after all. It can never be too perfect.

I wondered if I could have done anything differently which would have led me to be in a different situation, these thoughts took me back in time where it all began.

1
THIS IS HOW IT BEGINS

Summer 2008

It was one of the most boring summers I had in a very long time. There was nothing great about this vacation. My girlfriend Aarti and I had a falling apart. My school days were over and with that all my school friends left for their colleges. I was in a transition phase. All my life I wanted to make my life big. I wanted to be famous. I wanted to be the next Shah Rukh Khan. But now I had to settle for stepping into my dad's boots and going to a med school in Bombay. Perhaps Bombay was the only good part about it because I was told that it was the city where all your dreams could come true.

The summer was at its peak. There is this very peculiar thing about summers in Nagpur. They are here to stay. Temperatures soaring up to 48 degrees can actually roast up people who would consider it a joke. All my days were spent just lazing around the house and playing the same old stuff on my play station with my dog who would be my twin brother if he was human because he is as lazy as I am.

Nights were a bit troublesome. When I was in school I used to spend them talking on my cellphone to Aarti. Now since that was over I had nothing to do. I couldn't even get sleep because I had become a nocturnal creature following my one year stint with Aarti. We used to be one of those love birds teenagers who would spend their day at school together, drive back home together, meet up before and after tuitions and then get back together on the phone at night and retire into the night listening to each other, from telling each other how much you are in love with her...to singing songs for each other...to simply listening to the other person breathe as he fell asleep on the phone. All this may sound silly now but that was the routine. Thus getting through the day was easy but I would many a times find myself feeling nostalgic about those days and crying at nights. There is something about me that needs to be mentioned here-I'm a major weeper, I cry. May it be a good movie, a good book, a situation...I cry rivers. So this was probably too much to handle. So to make things easier I took up a part time job as a radio jockey on MY FM, the last shift. The job would require me to be on air from midnight to 3 AM. God knows how many people tuned in to listen but by the end of it I was generally too tired of listening to the same songs again and again and talking to nocturnal creatures like me that I would fall asleep as soon as I reached home and had no time to think.

Things were looking up with the day of me joining my med school drawing near. I was kind of looking forward to it because with that I would be changing my life altogether. New place, new friends, new girls and most of all a ray of hope that I would someday be the next SRK

2
B-TOWN KNOCKING

Summer 2008

Another day was dawning. The sound of the birds chirping could be heard at a distance. It was kind of strange because I live in a very urban area so such a thing was uncommon. It woke me up and I found out that it was my World Space Radio playing the song 'Aqueous Transmission' by Incubus. Although I really love the song and find it very peaceful, the part where it ends in birds chirping for 40 odd seconds is very disturbing. It was 7.30 AM and really early by my standards to be up in the morning. But now that I was awake I thought of finally having breakfast after ages. It had been months since I got up to the rising sun and my first meal would be lunch served to me in bed at 1 PM. That's the time my day would start. Today it felt surprisingly good to walk out to our lawn bare foot and see the people take a jog in the park outside my house. I decided to go and have breakfast at Gokul Vrindavan. It was a small South Indian joint few minutes walk from my place.

Although I hate South Indian food, the place served some great samosas. I love samosas. I can hog on them for life. So as I reached Gokul and placed my order and was slurping on my Pepsi with that long thin straw which is a trademark of all these small food joints, when my phone rang. It was Pritam Nyare a senior RJ from work who was calling. I had just met him once at the time of my audition and hadn't heard much from him since then. I received the call

'Hello'

'Hey Aman it's Pritam here'

'Hey wassup?'

'Nothing much. Sorry if I'm disturbing you. Were you sleeping?'

'No…I woke up early today. I was just finishing breakfast'

'That's good. Anyway there is some work which we need you for.'

'Ya…tell me…what is it?'

'There is this promotional event at Inox today for '*Bachna Aaye Hasino*' you know about it right'

'Yes I do. What about it?'

'Well Richa was supposed to anchor it but she has come down with fever so the boss was asking if you would be interested in stepping in for her'

'Hell ya… I would be interested…but are you sure about this. I mean it's a big job'

'Yes it is a big job and we think that you will be great to handle it and plus during your audition you said you wanna make it big in B

4

Town so the boss said why not start here. It's a good opportunity to interact with some people from the industry. Deepika Padukone, Ranbir Kapoor and Minisha Lamba are gonna be there with the director so don't screw it up'

'Thanks a lot. I won't screw this up don't worry'

'I know you won't. The event starts at two this afternoon so make sure you do some research and be well dressed and if you need some help call up Richa'

'Yes I will and thanks again'

'Don't thank me. Thank the bug that Richa caught. See you on the other side bro'

I was just spellbound I couldn't believe this was really happening. I called up my sis who lived in Bombay, she is an actress and had done a cameo in the same movie. She was playing Minisha's sis who gets married. She was delighted at the news and briefed me up on the story and some inside gossip to make things interesting. It was going to be great.

I finished my samosa, paid the waiter and dashed home. I had lot of work to do, the most important being looking good.

3
IT'S A NO SHOW

Summer 2008

'*Hum dono kudhko killer samajhte hai na. Par hum dono me kamiya hai. Hum dono perfect nahi hai.* That's why knowing you is like knowing myself. That's why we are made for each other. That's why I love you so much.' As Ranbir said these words to Deepika the rocking tune of *khuda jaane* came over and the credits flew up. That was the end of *bachna ae hasino*. I found myself leaving the theatre with Gogo our sound man from MY F.M. As I reached outside I felt my cellphone vibrating, it flashed Prateeksha didi calling.

'Hey how was it?'

'Hi dee the movie was nice...I saw you. You are looking damn pretty. I think this will help you with your big break.'

'Hey thank you. But tell me how the show was? I know you must have bowled over Deepika with your boyish charm'

'It was a no show dee... a no freaking show'

'Why what happened'

'They couldn't make it here. Ranbir had some work commitments and Deepika isn't making an appearance without him so that's that. It was all a waste'

'Hey don't be disheartened bro. Now you are coming to Bombay so you'll have your chances to meet people'

'I am counting on that sis. Anyway I'll be heading home now I'll catch up with you once I'm there.'

'Ya ok *chal* take care then bye.' So as I said that was it, I had a chance to make some contacts here and it all came down to nothing.

I bidded Gogo a goodbye and headed towards my bike when suddenly I heard someone call my name out. I turned around to see who it was. I saw this girl wearing a pink tank top with a denim jacket and a blue skirt waving at me. It was Riya, a junior of mine from school. She came over to me.

'Hey how are you RJ DODO?'

'Hey Riya what's up how are you?'

'I am good thank you…so you were here too to see Ranbir? Or let me guess Deepika right. I am such a big Ranbir fan and I'm so sad he couldn't come today'

'I was supposed to host the event just FYI. And ya I'm pretty sad about it myself.'

'Oh I see, all your hosting skills and all. It's been so long since I saw you'

'Ya I know three months.'

'Ya three months… ever since we gave you people a farewell. It has been a long time don't you think?'

'No actually it just feels like yesterday that I was in school and seeing you with that dude what's his name...uh...ya Palak it's all so fresh in my memory'

'Oh! you and your sarcasm. But seriously you had this big fan following in school for all your wit and your swimming achievements made it even better. All the girls would die to see you play soccer in the breaks and when you hosted the farewell and all it was fabulous.' Now all this flattering was getting to me...uhhh...Not really I kind of liked it.

'Wouldn't Palak be jealous if he knew you are flirting with me?'

'We broke up so that's not a problem. And just FYI I am not flirting I just admire you a lot. I listen to your show every night before I sleep.'

'Oh that's good but sorry to disappoint you... it's gonna come off AIR from tonight...you see I am leaving for college in three days so today is my last show'

'Oh that's so sad. Now I have to search for some other pastime at night...Anyway best of luck to you. By the way how is Aarti?'

'I don't know. We broke up three months ago'

'Oh...okay sorry for that. Anyway I was thinking if you are free now we can go grab a coffee or something'

'Riya actually...'

'Ya fine... no problem I know you are leaving and are keeping busy. It's fine. Take my number and call me if you're free sometime. Maybe then we can get some coffee.' I took down her number and gave her a missed call so she had mine.

'*Chalo* then you take care and best of luck with college and all and stay in touch'

'Ya definitely.'

With that she turned around called for a rickshaw and left. That was quite a meeting I thought. I knew I was popular and all in school but what she said really made me feel good about myself. I took my bike and headed home all the while thinking maybe coffee wouldn't have been such a bad idea after all.

4
THE LAST SHOW

Summer 2008

It was 11.50 at night. RJ Anubhav was doing his rounds of goodbyes for the night. I had around ten minutes before I went on AIR. Tonight was my last show and I was thinking about how I could make it special. The company had given me a nice farewell party some hours ago and I had managed to slip in some beers in my system. I wasn't high, just light headed and was feeling pretty good. I thought to myself that today I'm gonna go out there and have a fun time talking to my callers. But then the urgency of the situation struck me. I hadn't decided the topic of tonight's discussion. What was I gonna talk about. My day had been revolving around a lot of people whom I met at the party and before. But as I thought… the one person that stood out among the lot was Riya. And then it struck me. Tonight's topic was gonna be the one I had been avoiding for the past three months. Maybe

I wanted to avoid it. But now with those beers in my system maybe I could talk about it. Tonight's topic was going to be love.

I put on my headset, positioned myself at the console and took a deep breath. I heard Gogo through my headset 'going live in…3…2…1… go'

'Hello all the night creatures of Nagpur and welcome to your very own show Starry Starry Night with me RJ DODO. Today's show is very very special to me as it's been three months now since I have been doing this show. And today is also special because today will be the last time you will be listening to me. But don't worry. The show will go on as you are very special to us. Tonight is not about TRP's but about having a good time. Tonight we enjoy *kya pata kal ho na ho*. Ok so as we move on let me tell you about our topic for tonight. Tonight's topic is love and separation. I know you all love me and you are sad about me leaving so call me and let me know how you feel. You can also call me and tell me about your story of love and break ups. You can also call and tell me your views on love. Call me at 665566 and tell me what you feel. Till then this song for all of you because I love you'

And then I played the first song of the show 'Nothings Gonna Change My Love For You' by Glen Menderios. I have always loved this song and it was the perfect beginning to the show. As that song faded I had another treat for my listeners with the song '*Kal Ho Na Ho*' as I told you this show was about me… so I played this as this was my favorite song. I also love this movie which I have seen like 50 times. Anyway with this song coming to its end I had my first caller.

'Hello'

'*Helloji Dodoji bol rahe hai?*'

'*Ha ji aap kaun bol rahe hai*'

'*ji mera naam Manoj hai*'

'Manoji welcome to Starry Starry Nights'

'Thank you sir'

'*ji sir bataiye aap humko kya batana chahte hai*'

'*sir main aapko meri love story batana chahata hu*'

'*ha bataiye manoj ji*'

'*sir meri ek girlfriend hai woh delhi me hai. Main usse bahut love karta hu. Par wo bolti hai ki hume break lena chahiye kyuki hum bahut door rehte hai. Sir main apna ghar, job sab chodke uske pas gaya tha. Par wo phir bhi wapas nahi aayi. Sir uske bina yeh life bahut suni suni si lagti hai. Raat ko neend bhi nahi aati hai sir. Aapka show sunke bohot acha lagta hai ab aap bhi nahi rahenge to kya karenge*'

I was really touched by this guy's story and had no words yet I had to manage

'*Manoj ji hum sab aapka dard samajhte hai. Aapne apne pyar ke liye itna sub kiya iske liye* hats off to you. *Par aaj main manoj ji and* everybody listening out there *ko ek baat batana chahata hu.* Guys this life is yours. It's been given to you to make it big… not in months and years but make it big with the deeds you do. Everyone will not understand you but never give up on life as it always has something better for you'

Wow!! That was pretty intense! I never knew I had it in me or was it just the beer. Anyway, '*aur manoj ji ab main jaa raha hu toh kya hua kal se ek hot ladki yeh show host karegi unko sun kar aapko aur maja aayega.* Thank you for calling. Anyone else feels like sharing their story call me. *Tab tak yeh gaane* just for you'

As I played 'Roobaroo' from Rang De Basanti I started to think how tough life gets on people when it comes to love. This guy quit his job, his life for a girl who didn't even love him. Does love really hold a position before yourself. Does love really means so much that nothing else in your life matters. Does such kind of love really exist? And if it does how do you know that it has happened.

The show moved on, people called me and told me a lot of things. There were people who told me about the person they love but how he didn't know. There were people who told me how love is a complete waste of time. There were people who told me how they found their true love and how their life was perfect. From first love to lost love I heard it all. The songs kept playing and calls kept coming, it was all routine till this call came. I saw the number flashing. I knew this number. I knew it too well. I never thought I would get a call from her after how we parted ways. The nostalgia, it was all coming back to me. I couldn't ignore the call. It was AARTI.

5

I HAVE BECOME...COMFORTABLY NUMB

March 2008

It was one of those evenings for me and Aarti. The birds were flying back home after a long day. On the horizon the setting sun was making love to the water. We sat on the cliff next to the Ambazari Lake like we had so many times before. Close to each other, her head on my shoulder just looking at the sun going down. I knew by then I loved this girl. I knew I wouldn't mind spending the rest of my life with her. I knew she was the one for me and she was the one there ever will be. I just didn't want this to end. But how would I have known then that everything you wish for isn't what you always get.

'Aman do you see that boat at the end of the lake. I doubt I have ever seen it before'

'Yes I know, but then we are just too lost in each other to notice anything else sweetheart'

'You know I was wondering that perhaps our life is just like that boat.'

'You think so? What happened to you? Comparing our life to a boat has to have a deep meaning'

'Ok forget the boat I'll put it out for you in simple words. You and I just cannot work out.'

'What! What are you talking about I just don't get you'

'Listen you are going to go away to Bombay in a few months and I will be going to Manipal. There is no future of this relationship. I know right now we are all about each other and you will say that you love me and all but come on Aman we are just 18… just out of school. We seriously have to move on. I think we should break up. Spend some time away from each other. I know it's going to be tough for you and believe me it's going to be very hard for me too. But once we get used to it I think we will do just fine.'

I was just out of words. As shocked as I was having heard all this I was disgusted that all of what I had been thinking just a few minutes ago had all come down to this. The dream world that I was building had come crashing down on the reality. I felt like my heart was beating so fast my chest would explode. My head was in turmoil and my eyes had tears. Yet the way Aarti had done this and the way she was still so composed about it made me smile. All I could say to her then was 'As you wish.' She gave me a peck on my cheek as she got up to leave. Maybe that was her way of saying goodbye. On 4th March 2008 she left me all by myself on that cliff showing me that all good things do come to an end.

July 2008

That was three months ago. Today the same girl had called me up on my radio show to tell me something about love. All I could be is surprised about how life could be so ironic. I tried my best to sound normal.

'Hello who is this?'

'Hi Aman this is Aarti.'

'Hey Aarti! Welcome to Starry Starry Nights. So tell me what do you have to tell us today?'

'How are you Aman?'

'I am good, thank you Aarti. How are you tonight?

'I am fine Aman.'

'Ok just to let you know I feel very weird when people call me by my real name on radio. Anyway what is it that you want to tell us tonight?'

'I had a boyfriend, we broke up three months back. I think he was very hurt when I broke up with him. Tonight I just want to tell him that I loved him a lot. I just want to know how he is. I want to tell him that all these three months there hasn't been a day I have not thought of him. I really miss him and I would love to hear from him. I know after all I have done I am asking for a bit too much but if he is listening I want him to please call me and get back in touch if only as a friend. I really miss him'

'Aarti I see what you are saying but if you loved him so much why did you break up with him in the first place? This is what I want to tell everyone listening. Never let go of someone who loves you because there is nothing else that feels as amazing as the feeling of being in love.'

'I was stupid. He was going to go away to college and I thought this long distance relationship won't work. I always thought that it is better to let go of someone who loves you…than keeping him…in love with you…when you know you just can't be with him. I was wrong. I am sorry.'

'Okay Aarti we will convey your message and thank you for calling Starry Starry Nights. And here is a song just for you.'

I didn't know what to play. I had to play something. I played "November Rain by Gunz N Roses". What was I supposed to do? Was I supposed to just forget all of what had happened? Was I to think that all that never happened? Was I to call her and say 'hey sweetheart everything is just fine and I forgive you.' I didn't know what I was going to do. Right now the song was fading and I had a last call which I had to attend.

'Hello! Who is this?'

'Hey Dodo, it's me Riya.'

'Oh! Hi Riya how are you?'

'I am fine thank you.'

'So tell me what do you want to tell us tonight?'

'Tonight I just want to thank you on the behalf of the entire city of Nagpur for being with us through your show. And I just want to tell you that we all love you a lot.'

'Thanks a lot Riya. I really appreciate it.'

'Have a nice life in Bombay Aman.'

'Thank you so much. And this last song of the night is for all of you.'

With that I played "Dosti by KK" and left the console bid goodbye and headed towards my bike in the parking lot. Thoughts of Aarti were still fresh in my mind. My cell phone rang, it was Daniel calling

'Hello'

'Hey bro I heard your show tonight. So are you going to call her?'

Daniel and I were in school together and he knew about me and Aarti.

'I don't know dude.'

'Dude come on she apologized to you on All India Radio and you say I don't know. Come on I think you should call her.'

'Listen Danny it is pretty late and I need to get back home and get some sleep. I am leaving town in two days. And as far as Aarti goes I will think about it.'

'Suit yourself but I think you should call her. Anyway, goodnight.'

'Goodnight.'

As I headed home I was thinking whether I should call her up and say that everything was fine. Or was it just my ever so interfering ego that was stopping me from calling her. Whatever it was it could wait tonight. It had been a long day and I was calling it a night.

The next two days just passed by in no time. And it was finally the day I left for Bombay. Mom and Dad dropped me off at the airport. And after all those hugs and kisses I went in and checked in. I spent my time before my flight just listening to some music on my phone and drinking my can of Diet Coke. Finally the departure of my flight was called and I boarded the flight. After placing my hand baggage in the overhead compartment I took my seat by the window and was just going to switch my cell phone off when it rang. It was Daniel calling.

'Hey Danny boy perfect timing. I was just going to switch my phone off as I am on board and leaving. Good to see you called to say bye.'

'Oh so you are on the flight already!'

'Yes where else would I be?'

'Aman I got to tell you something.'

'Yes tell me.'

'It is about Aarti.'

'Oh come on Daniel can't this wait.'

'I don't think it can. Aarti is no more. She met with an accident while driving back from her morning jog. She died on the spot.'

'Is this some kind of a cheap joke to make me call her because believe me it's not funny.'

'It's no joke Aman. And now you are just late. You should have called her.'

I hung up. Everything around me just blurred out. I felt numb. My mind was racing back to the time I spent with Aarti. From the evenings by the lake to the rides back home. I could see everything flashing me by as the plane rolled on the runway. Danny was right, I should have called her. I should have told her that everything was fine. But now when I thought about it maybe there wasn't much I could have done. I still remember what she said to me the other day on the radio show 'it is better to let go of someone who loves you…than keeping him… in love with you, when you know you just can't be with him'

I can never forget these words as in some way these are the words that define me today. Maybe she was right.

6
A NEW LIFE

Bombay Rains 2008

'Ladies and gentlemen welcome to Mumbai's Chatrapati Shivaji International Airport…the outside temperature is 27 degree Celsius. We hope you have a pleasant stay in Mumbai…thank you for choosing Jet Lite.' The air hostess announced.

I was here. Mumbai…I was in Mumbai. The city of dreams…the business capital of India. A city where more than a thousand people come every day to fulfill their dreams. Some come here to get a job. Some come here to make it in movies. Some come here to become Sachin Tendulkar. Well as for the rest they just come here in search for a better life. Everybody just wants to make a name for himself. Everybody just wants to make it big. For some of them their dreams do get shape and turn into reality. But for the others…what can I say…I guess Mumbai happens to them. As for me…I was just a guy who had come here to get his Bachelor's degree in Medicine and

Surgery. But somewhere within me too there was this boy with stars in his eyes and a dream that someday I might become the next Shah Rukh Khan.

I claimed my baggage and hired a taxi and was soon travelling along the streets of Mumbai. Everything seemed to be so fast here. Everyone seemed to be in so much of a hurry; speeding vehicles on the Western Express highway. People running across roads before the signal turned red again making their way to board those overcrowded trains which looked as if they would break down anytime. Something like a traffic jam created such a ruckus amongst people like the world was coming to an end. Over the years that I have spent in Mumbai I can describe the city as...*yeh sheher me ek apna hi nasha hai.* Mumbai to me is like indigenous liquor. We drink it all in...it may not always go down smooth...you may love it you may hate it...but once you are addicted to it...you can't live without it. I had been born and brought up in Nagpur where I had lived all my life until now. Nagpur was a city which ran at its own dilly dally pace; a place where if you had to meet someone at five you would have to tell that person to be ready at four. And even if that person did manage to get ready by four for your meeting and you got late...well who cares...its Nagpur after all. So the sheer presence of the quick pace of this city thrilled me. I remember that I was travelling in cab on the Vashi Bridge enjoying the view outside the bay that divides Mumbai from Navi Mumbai when I got the first feel of the Bombay rains. It was marvelous. All of a sudden it had started to rain heavily. Ever since I was a little child I think I have always had immense love for the rains. And as I grew up rains have always been associated with happy memories; my first bike ride, my first national swimming gold medal, my first goal by a bicycle kick, the first time I proposed a girl and she said yes and my first kiss. All these memories and much more made rain such an integral part of my life. Therefore this truly was a treat. It seemed like Mumbai was welcoming me with open arms; that great things were in store for me. And all I did was lean out of that cab window and drink it all in. Although the blaring horns of those stupid trucks with their retarded HORN OK PLEASE signs made this moment very short for me…I was happy. Well as a matter of 'I was happy' would definitely be an understatement. I was delighted…delighted to be in Mumbai. After about an hour's drive I reached my destination. Nerul, Dr. D.Y.Patil Medical College and Hospital. The place I would call home for the next five and a half years. That is of course if I didn't flunk any year.

The thirteen storied building stood in front of me. The college was up to the sixth floor and from the seventh floor was where boys the hostel began. I took the elevator and went up to the seventh floor where I had been allotted my hostel room. For a medical college hostel the place was pretty quiet. I went up to my room, room number 733 and unlocked the door. As I entered the room I was greeted by a guy who was setting up his table with books.

'Hello. You must be Aman…I am Krish Tandon your room mate.' He said

The guy was short…I guess about 5 ft 7inches as opposed to my 5 ft 10. He had jet black spiky hair which looked as if they were done by a very good hair dresser. He wore green Tag Heuer spectacles…the same ones that Ranbir Kapoor had worn in *Bachna*

Ae Hasino. He had stubble that really went with his personality. He wasn't well built or what some people may call in shape…I think from all standards he looked really malnourished. But there was something about him…maybe it was his confidence or the way he was carrying himself that I thought both of us are going to hit off just fine. In other words I think I was thankful to god for giving me a roommate who wasn't a complete freak.

'Hi Krish…it's nice meeting you.' I said.

'Well same here man.' And he talks in good English…great.

'So where are you from?' I asked

'I'm from Delhi…Noida. What about you?'

'I am from Nagpur.'

'Oh nice…the orange city huh…hopefully we will share a lot of oranges over the next few years.' He said.

'Sure dude…so when did you get here?'

'Well I reached Bombay last night…I stayed over at a relative's place…reached college a few hours ago.' He said.

'Well it seems you have brought all your books and all.' I said after looking around the room which already had all his stuff unpacked and put up properly.

'Ya as a matter of fact I bought them back in Delhi itself…my dad knows the owner of the Bookshop so I got a healthy discount.'

'Good for you man.'

'Hey I hope you are fine with that bed by the window…I'm sorry I already set mine up on the other one.' He said.

'Are you kidding me…it's perfect…anyway I hear that the building outside this window is the girl's hostel...lovely view every night...right.' I winked. 'So anyway tell me what the schedule for today is.'

'Well today being our first day there is no official college...we have an orientation class where all of us will be addressed by the dean and then all the head of the departments will take us for a tour showing us where classes will be held and the practical halls. They will also tell what books are to be referred...it's there at 2 PM.' There was an evident tone of excitement in his voice.

'Sounds great...well maybe after that we can go to the book shop and I can buy my books too.'

'Ya sure.'

I unpacked my suitcases and arranged all my clothes in the cupboard that was there in the room. I set up my bed and placed all my bathroom products in the bathroom. I washed my face and changed out of my capris and Puma T-shirt into a black shirt and dark blue denims. I had a final look at my face in the mirror. I was happy with the way I looked and was ready to go on with my first day of college. There was still some time in hand so I & Krish got to talking. We talked about our schools and our hobbies. That is when I found out that he played the guitar. I had always wanted to learn to play the six strings so I thought that now I might finally learn it from Krish. We talked about the kind of music we liked and it was great to know that both of us more or less listened to the same shit. We talked about how the hostel was nothing less than a three star hotel...not like the ones in the Government medical colleges where there is a common toilet and bathroom for one floor. Here we had attached

Bathrooms in every room. The rooms had ACs and proper beds and tables. There was another similarity in the both of us…we had already fallen in love with the college.

Soon it was 2 PM and it was time for orientation. We went down to the third floor Lecture hall . Krish and I took seats next to each other in the fourth row of the lecture hall so that we wouldn't be perceived as the first row geeks by the class or the last row chronic bunkers by the professors. As I sat there I took a look around the hall and was really impressed with the way it had been made. It felt more like those multiplex movie theatres than a lecture hall. It had three screens…one in the center up front and one on each side somewhere in the middle with LCD projectors put up on the wall. I was so glad that I had finally come a long way from blackboard learning. At that time I couldn't wait to call my friends back home and tell them that my college truly seemed like the best thing that had ever happened to me. My eyes were wandering and they finally started scanning each and every person in the room. I had thought that since the college is in Mumbai the crowd will be really amazing…but to my disappointment it seemed nowhere close to that. Everyone just looked so dull and boring. I did spot people who looked cool but I guess they had a negative aura around them that made me think that perhaps finding nice friends around here was going to be tough. The girls too were just weird…I mean yes there were some decent looking girls who might have been of my interest…but all in all I was pretty let down. As I was just wrapping up on the class scanning that is when my eyes caught someone. She was a girl sitting in the second row. I couldn't see her face then…she was surrounded by three or four other girls who kept talking to her all the time. From what I could see she had long hair which reached up to her waist that were tied up is a pony revealing her fair neck. *Palat Palat Palat* (turn around I wanna see your face) I kept saying to myself. But she did not turn around. She was too busy talking to those girls around her…it seemed like nothing else mattered to her at that point of time. Damn those stupid girls. Who is she? What is her name? I wanted to go up in front and have a look at her and maybe say hi or something…but then that would have seemed desperate. Five and a half years…I had a lot of time. Soon the orientation began.

It began with the Dean of our college Dr. Mrs. Solanki welcoming our entire batch to the college. She told us about the basic rules that we were to follow when in college. It included basics like being well mannered…being well dressed…greeting the professors etc etc. She also told us that as a law passed by the government of India ragging of any sort will not be tolerated and we should make it a point to report any case of ragging to the college authorities…and that the college would take strict actions against those who involve in that act…well so much for hollow words I thought. Then she introduced us to all the head of the departments. In the first year of our degree we were supposed to study three subjects… first was Anatomy and the HOD was Dr.Manjrekar. He was in his late forties. He came up to the mic and introduced himself and cracked a rather crappy joke which surprisingly everyone found funny. I for once didn't see the whole point in his joke but still I thought I should give it to the man for being such a jolly fellow. I mean I seriously liked the guy and thought to myself that during his days he must have been a major crowd puller and he was the only HOD who actually dressed up as if he were a doctor. The second subject was physiology…its HOD was Mrs.Heda. A woman who seemed as old as my grandmother who was definitely more than 80 years old. The third subject was biochemistry; the HOD's name was Mrs.Kanitkar, a woman who hadn't as much changed her expression ever since she had entered the room some thirty minutes back. And even when she was asked to come to the podium and address the batch all she did was sit in her chair with that frustrated expression on her face and waved it off. LOL LOL LOL was all that was going in my head after seeing her.

After this we were divided into three groups on the basis of our CET ranks and sent with one HOD each to their respective departments. I being in the first fifty was in group one and was supposed to go to the Anatomy department. Krish was in group three and was going to the biochemistry department. It was when we were all finally leaving the lecture theatre that I did finally see her. She looked as if she were an angel fallen from heaven itself. Beautiful…gorgeous…pretty…these aren't even the appropriate words to describe her. If I still have to put it in words all I can say is…divine beauty. Fair…oh she was fair…she was fairer than snow white. Her hair was black and long tied in a pony with fringes on her forehead that made her look like a doll. The way she carried herself was nothing but elegance personified. She was not one of those cute girls you just wanna hug nor was she one of the hot babes whom you can go on ogling till the end of time she was just out of this world. She was one girl who could on any day make any girl envious of her and any guy fall head over heels for her. As I said she was divine. And she was going to the physiology department so I still couldn't go up to her. Again I thought to myself, five and a half years Aman…you have a lot of time.

The tours were great, pretty informative. We were all shown around the college and department. The practical halls were superbly made. The professors were very friendly and they told us all the books that would help us do well in exams. Thus the two hours we spent touring the college did not seem like a complete waste. Finally after I was done with my last department I got a call from Krish and we decided to go to The National Bookshop next to LP Petrol Pump to get my books. It was a ten minute walk from my college and we walked through the campus. The campus was fabulous. It had an Amphitheatre, a sports academy which consisted of a cricket stadium which could seat over fourty five thousand people. There was a state of the art swimming pool, four tennis courts, two basketball courts, two indoor badminton courts and squash courts. The gym was well made and it had a steam and sauna facility. Well I do remember watching the finals of the Indian Premier League or the IPL as they call it. It was held in this very stadium which was situated right in my college campus. This was really cool, I thought to myself. Finally we reached the bookshop and there I saw her again. She was with her gang of girls and had finished buying her books when I reached. She and her friends took an auto rickshaw and went away. I missed her again. I bought my books which included three volumes of BD Chaurasia and three volumes of Cunningham's for Anatomy, one Guyton and one Sembulingam for Physiology also one Satyanarayan's Essentials of Biochemistry. I was really grateful to Krish for coming along with me because the bags got very heavy and there was no way I could have carried them on my own. I guess I got my first taste of the burden of MBBS.

After having a quick lunch which consisted of two masala dosas and one Thumbs up at Rangoli family restaurant both of us got back to the hostel. As we were going back to our room we came across two seniors who were playing cricket in the corridor. The short and stout guy was Shivam and the tall and muscular guy was Haider, which of course I know now but at that time to us they were just *Bhaiya*.

'Hello *bhaiya*.' Both I and Krish greeted them.

'Oh ho! freshers?' both of them said in unison. They had a sense of lust in their eyes, it could be compared to that of a rapist as he stalks his prey.

'Yes *bhaiya*.' We replied.

'Good…Good…you go to your room now…we will meet for real at night.' The way they said it made us feel like we were really going to get molested that night.

We went to our room. I set up my table with the books I had brought. And then I and Krish both decided to take a nap. We woke up at 9 PM and went to the canteen on the ground floor for dinner. The food was pathetic. The paneer tasted stale and the rotis were undercooked. We were having a tough time putting it down our throats. That is when this guy walked up to us.

'Hi…my name is Madhur Verma…how do you do.' Huh what…I thought to myself and I guess Krish thought the same because both of us returned him blank looks. 'Both of you are first year's right…I saw you in orientation today, I'm Madhur.' Well that was much better I thought.

'Hi Madhur, my name is Krish and this is Aman. Please have a seat.' Krish said pulling up a chair for him.

'Hey guys nice to meet you.' He said as he sat down next to Krish.

'So Madhur where are you from?' I asked trying not to seem impolite.

'I am from Delhi, Gurgaon. What about you.'

'Well I am from Nagpur. But Krish here is too from Delhi, Noida.' I said nudging Krish.

'Oh that's great.' He said.

Soon Krish and Madhur got talking about Delhi and how it was so different from Mumbai. They talked about their schools and common friends they had there. It was definitely a conversation I was not interested in but I looked at both of them very intently picking up certain words like Delhi Public School RK Puram and MMS scandal in the process. Well after dinner all of us went back to the hostel. Krish went with Madhur to his room to check it out and I came back to smy room. I opened my Cunningham's Dissection Manual volume one and started going through it. Mr.Manjrekar had told us to go through the first fifteen pages of the book to get a hang of how things would be. I found it pretty interesting and within twenty minutes I was done reading the allotted pages. I decided to take a look outside the window in my room at the girl's hostel building. I was hoping I would get a sight of that girl again. All the curtains of all the rooms were drawn closed and all I could see were shadows behind them. Soon Krish came back to the room and Madhur was with him.

'Dude what the fuck…you have been studying?' Krish said looking at the book kept open on my bed.

'Ya I was. The HOD asked us to go through the first fifteen pages that's why.' I replied.

'Oh ya…I read the first thirty pages of that book at home itself and believe me it's a complete waste of time. That book is ancient…I mean who the fuck reads Cunningham's these days.' Krish said.

'Well I don't know about that. I mean I was just doing what I was asked to do. It did in a way seem interesting.' I meekly protested.

'That's bullshit dude. Anyway fuck that you guys tell me whats up with you both I mean do you have any girlfriends back home.' Oh now we're talking…the guy talk…cool I thought.

'No…none here' I thought talking about Aarti just yet wouldn't be appropriate. 'What about you Madhur.'

'No re…no girlfriends…never had one as a matter of fact.' I was pretty surprised at the response. I mean the guy was fair…tall…about six feet tall…had a nice face, sharp features and according to what most girls would say was pretty handsome. I somehow expected him to have had a couple of girlfriends during his school days.

'Why so? I mean are you the guy who believes in true love and all and you haven't found the right one yet.' Well that was the only possible reason I could think of at that time.

'Na…nothing like that…It was just that I was very fat in my school days…what you see me as today is just because I have been working out in the gym for the past one year. But back in school I weighed 110 kgs and looked like a real nerd.' No…that can't be possible I thought. I mean I couldn't believe this guy standing in front of me right now was fat and undesirable at some point of time. And I guess even Krish agreed with me. To lay doubts at rest he did take out a photo of himself from his wallet and showed it to us. It was about a year old. And yes he was right…he was big and overweight. The transformation he had gone through in a year was really commendable, I mean seriously hats off to him. He told us that he kept that photo of his in his wallet to remind him of what he used to be and how he had come a long way from there. 'So Krish, what about you, do you have any?' he asked Krish.

'No…I just broke up with my girlfriend before coming to Mumbai. Well I didn't really love her and she was going to go to college in Delhi itself so I did not see the point in continuing with it.' He was very straight forward with his answer. 'So did any of you see any girls in our batch you might be interested in.' he asked.

'Well it's too early to tell…don't you think.' Madhur said.

'No I mean now that we are friends I think we should set up the Bro code.' Krish said

'Bro Code…what the fuck is that?' I asked

'Well it's like if you like a girl you tell us… and none of us except you will pursue her…until you are turned down if there is a conflict of interest.' Krish explained. 'So…is there anyone?'

'Ya that sounds fair…and no none for me… anyway I think the girls in our batch are pretty lame.' Madhur said.

'And what about you Aman…have you seen anyone who you might be interested in.' Krish narrowed his eyes on me. What should I do…I thought. Should I just tell them about this mystery girl whose name I didn't know? Should I mark my territory in the BRO CODE?

'Well there is this girl I do fancy.' I decided to tell them. 'I don't know her name… but she is fair…like really fair. I have never seen some one as beautiful as her in my entire life. She was wearing a pink tank top today…was surrounded by three or four other girls. She was wearing red sneakers' I tried my best to draw her out for them.

'Oh yes…that girl with the red shoes. I know her. Her name is Aisha Rahim…we used to be in tuitions together. She is from Delhi too. The entire college has been talking about her I hear. I met some seniors in the evening and they too were asking me about her. The girl in the red shoes… that's exactly how everyone is describing her.' Madhur said. 'It's so funny you know…I was with her in the same tuitions for two years and I never found her that attractive. I mean sure people used to go gaga over her all the time but to me I thought she was this girl with a lot of attitude. I never really liked her so much. She was dating this guy called Rehan back then. I don't know if they are still together. He was a big show off and filthy rich. She was his trophy girlfriend. I guess she is all beauty no brains. And if I were you I wouldn't get my hopes up with her because according to me even if she is single she would go out with a guy who can really spend a lot on her. I mean she is kind of high maintenance.' Madhur was shattering my hopes with his words and for some reason I didn't like it. I guess maybe when reality does smack you in the face…it hurts. He was right I thought. I mean she is way out of my league. I know I am not great looking or anything. I have just about average looks. I don't have a hot body and I am not even that rich. And plus now I was in Bombay. Nobody knew me over here. I was a nobody. Well sure if I would have been in Nagpur things would have worked differently. People over there knew me. National gold medalist...Radio jockey...Brilliant sense of humor...I had a lot of things to work my way with the chicks there. Here I could have as well just walked passed a bunch of people and nobody would have noticed me. Well I just decided to go with Madhur's words and drop the entire thought about Aisha with whom a few hours ago I was building a castle of dreams. Then finally Krish told us about this girl named Gurlyn he had met in the orientation. He told us whatever information he knew about her, it included stuff like she lived in Abu Dhabi and was originally from Punjab and that she was really cute and he fancied her. So the Bro Code was formed. Since that day Gurlyn would be Krish's territory and Aisha would be my territory although now I thought it was a complete waste but still who knows what could happen. Madhur for now was a freelancer.

We were still talking and Madhur was telling us how he is not used to staying away from his family and was feeling homesick when someone knocked at the door. It was a guy who introduced himself as Shreenivas and told us that we were all called in the hostel's common hall by the seniors. It suddenly reminded me of that look which Shivam *bhaiya* had in his eyes when we had met them in the evening. It was time for our first ragging session. I swear to god I had never been as scared as I was then.

We stood there in the hall in a line. We were five people...I, Krish, Madhur Shreenivas and Hari. There was another line in front of us facing us. That line had ten people. We were out numbered. They all were laughing and it looked as if they were having a gala time among themselves. We on the other hand stood there with our hands behind our backs and looked as if we were punished by someone. Finally a huge guy stepped forward from there line and told us that what was going to happen today was not ragging. It was a PDP…Personality Development Program. As I heard this I giggled a little. All the seniors looked at me ferociously. I realized that I had committed a huge mistake which could have cost me my life.

'*Kyu Hasi aa rahi hai?* What is so funny huh? Is this a comedy show going on here? Do I look like Navjot Singh Sidhu to you?' the guy sounded darnn serious. I shook my head and looked down. He continued 'See what we're going to do today is not ragging…it is no where close to ragging. We are not going to ask you to strip and get naked and all. We all belong from good families here and we know that such kind of behavior is unacceptable. It's just going to be healthy interaction where we might ask you to do certain things like sing and dance. If anyone of you is uncomfortable with this he is free to leave right now. But if you decide to stay and then go out and complain about us to the college authorities then consider yourself dead.' I should back out I thought to myself. It's not worth the risk, I should totally go. But I found no support from anyone so I decided to stay.

'Very well then. Now first of all each one of you will have to come ahead chance by chance and give your introduction. Your intro should consist of your name, your parents' name, where you are from, the name of your school, and your hobbies. After that if we have any questions for you we will ask you. Is that clear?'

'Yes Sir' we all said.

'Oye don't call me Sir…don't call any of your seniors sir unless they are your teachers. Don't you know that addressing your seniors as sir is also a kind of ragging? And we are not ragging you…this is a PDP. Call us *Bhaiya.* Is that clear?'

'Yes *Bhaiya.*'

So it began. All of us went ahead one by one and gave our intro. Surprisingly it was going pretty well. Everyone was enjoying the light hearted comments being passed at people and it was all in good spirit. We ourselves were having fun. I was glad I had decided to stay. When all of us were done we were asked to do something called the fresher's salute. I should tell you that this fresher's salute was the most obscenely hilarious thing I had ever come across. It was very innovative according to me. All of us had to put our right hand on our forehead as if we were saluting. With our left hand we had to hold our crotch. And we had to hop in one place while uttering some really vulgar words. Well if I had to translate the wordings of the fresher's salute for you in English they would sound like…I'm some Tom Dick and Harry…I trim my pubic hair…I'm a condom…a penile lubricant…and I present my smooth and shiny ass in front of my seniors. And as we said the last part we had to turn around bend over and point our asses towards them. It was really funny. And the hardest part was to do it with a straight face because if you laughed or smiled while doing it you had to repeat it. This really was crazy ass fun. After this we were asked to either sing a song or do a dance depending on whatever we wanted to. I sang the song 'Bhula Do' by Raeth. It was well appreciated. But the real star of that night was Madhur who danced to the song *Choli ke peeche kya hai*. I thought he danced like a cheap whore but I guess that is what is needed to cheer up a bunch of drunken people. Anyway after all this, all of us had a nice talk with all the seniors and they told us that if we needed any help we were free to come and ask them. They told us which professors were good and which lectures were worth attending. Finally after two hours of ragging…oh no sorry…PDP…we dispersed.

It was 1 AM and I had to wake up early the next morning as the first lecture was at 9 AM so I decided to call it a night. As I lay down on my bed I reviewed in my head the happenings of the day. I had found good friends in Krish and Madhur even though it had been just one day, I knew that I could really click with these two guys. My seniors were nice and helpful, at least that was my first impression. The college was amazing and I was really happy to be here. And finally my thought rested on Aisha. Well to some extent I thought Madhur was right and I should just not think about it. I mean it was just yesterday that I had found out about Aarti being no more. I should think more about making a reputation for myself here I thought. I hailing from a small city like Nagpur was definitely going to have some problem fitting in with the big city guys. I definitely did not want myself to be alienated. Being the crowd puller that I always had been I was not ready to change that part of my life. Beginning from tomorrow I would talk to everyone and be a very social person. Beginning from tomorrow Aman Sarin is going to go out there and start conquering the hearts of everyone in his batch. He was gonna start a new life in Mumbai. With that thought I drifted off to sleep looking forward to the next morning.

7

AN EXPOSED JUGULAR

Bombay Rains 2008

The next morning I got up to a rainy day. As I walked down the corridor to the water cooler to get some water I could really see why Bombay rains are to die for. The rain was pouring down heavily on Bombay. There are these mountains that you see as you pass on the Thane Belapur highway which is just next to my college. Well, that day I couldn't see those mountains. It seemed as it was some PC Sorkar's magic trick which had made them disappear. The clouds had decended down and as I stood on the seventh floor of our building and looked out, the entire sky looked misty and foggy. The rains made everything even more magical. I got some water from the cooler and got back to my room. Krish was out of bed by then and he was standing outside the room smoking a cigarette. He hadn't said he smoked, so obviously I was a little shocked.

'Dude…you smoke.'

'Oh ya dude…I need one every morning…without it I can't get the pressure to shit.' He said.

'That is the first time I have heard anyone say that…how long have you been smoking for.'

'Well I started when I was in eleventh grade, back then I was a chronic smoker but now I just need one to shit and one after every meal.'

'Ah okay.' I said. I guess I was a little annoyed at him. I had a reason though…all my life I had been someone who thought smokers were bad people. They ruin their own life and the lives of everyone around them. And now I was friends with a smoker. Forget that, I was going to share a room with a smoker, the thought only added to my frustration, but I didn't mention anything.

I went inside and got on with my morning business. It took me around half an hour to get done with things and at around 8 AM I had bathed and was ready for the real first day of college. I told Krish who had entered the bathroom that I was going down for breakfast and would meet him there. I met Madhur along the way and together we went to canteen. We placed our order at the counter and took a table near the entrance of the canteen. As we were waiting for the guy to get our order I saw Aisha walking towards the canteen with her girl gang. She was wearing a yellow tank top today and blue faded jeans, she carried a red umbrella and of course those red sneakers. My eyes followed her as she entered the canteen, bought a bottle of water and left the canteen with all her followers. Gosh! she was so beautiful and she was so out of my league…damn!. I turned around and saw Madhur looking at me with a wicked expression.

'What' I asked

'Aakho me teri ajab si ajab si adaiye hai...oh ho ho...aakho me teri' he started singing that song from Om Shanti Om where Shah Rukh gets lost in a dream world after seeing Deepika. I knew why he was singing that song.

'Just shut up man' I said

'Ok fine...anyway tell me...what are you going to do dude? Are you going to ask her out or what?'Madhur said.

'Dude are you crazy or what? She doesn't even know my name. Forget the name, she doesn't even know I exist. I can't just go up to her and say...hi my name is Aman and I have the hots for you...will you be my girlfriend...because I think you are the most beautiful girl to have ever step foot on the face of earth. It does not work that way.' I blabbered.

'Obviously I know that it doesn't work that way...you are not having a conversation with a sixth grader you see.' He said.

'Oh I know that...I'm just having it with some dumbfuck who has never had a girlfriend.' I said this with an evident sarcastic tone but somewhere I knew I had hit the wrong buttons. 'Dude I'm sorry ya...I was just pulling your leg...I have this bad habit of being sarcastic all the time.' I apologized instantly.

'Oh don't worry about it...I know you were being sarcastic...but in a way you are right. I won't be the best guy to take relationship advice from.' He had a disappointed tone in his voice. I guess I had brought back some bad memories with my words. I felt sorry...I really did. I really liked this guy...it was time I did some damage control.

'Dude you don't worry okay. I know within no time you are going to be one of the most popular guy in college. I'm very good at predicting future. Well I can't predict my own future but other people's future, I'm pretty spot on with. And what I see of you is that you are going to be surrounded by chicks all the time. I can't say if any of them will be good looking or not but still you will do great.' I was really trying hard to cheer him up.

'Dude don't bull shit me…you don't even have a crystal ball to tell you that.'

'*Arre* I don't need a crystal ball, this is a very different type of astrology. In this I predict a person's future based on his nature, his personality and the way he goes around handling people.' I was really bull shitting him.

'Ok Mr.Hotshot Astrologer, tell me where Krish will be based on your observation.' Oh my God I thought…he was even buying my crap.

'Well Krish will be fine but eventually he will find someone who he would want to spend his entire life with and will retreat into his own happy bubble.'

'You know Aman, that is the worst attempt anyone must have made to cheer someone up.' He said.

'Ya I know. I think I went a little over the top with Krish right.'

'Ya hehe…happy bubble…where do you even come up with such crap.'

'Well I guess three months of being an RJ teaches you to be full of crap.'

'You were an RJ…where…when?'

'Dude there are so many things about me you don't know. Anyway it's time for the lecture, we should get going.'

'Ya…don't wanna be late on the first day.'

We went up to the lecture hall. Krish was already there and had saved seats for us. The first lecture was Anatomy. Mr Manjrekar our HOD himself took the lecture. He taught us about the general considerations of Anatomy. It included stuff like the types of bones…different parts of bones…types of fascia…bursa…etc etc. I developed an instant liking toward the way he taught things and in turn I developed a liking towards him. He had a certain zeal with which he taught things, he taught with a lot of enthusiasm, he simplified everything to the very basics which made getting the hang of things very easy for us. In between his lectures he used to come up with the most downright stupid jokes I had ever heard but it helped in keeping the mood light and made attending his lectures fun. The second lecture of that day was also anatomy and it was taken by Dr.D'Souza. He had a very different approach towards teaching than Mr.Manjrekar had. He believed in cutting everything down to the facts. These were facts which if you jotted down and reproduced them as they were on the answer sheet no one could stop you from passing anatomy with flying colors. The lecture was on breasts. When we were young…breast to us were organs to feed newly born babies. After we reached our teens and got used to a world beyond Cartoon Network and POGO they became the source of lots of our fantasies and solo flying sessions. But by the time this lecture got over all they were to me were organs with a vast blood supply, some absolutely ridiculous lymphatic drainage, which had relations to stuff in the human body that I couldn't even spell correctly. It was really surprising how something like breasts that were so fascinating for those fifty odd guys sitting in that classroom and I guess maybe for some girls too was converted into something that all of them would hate for the next one year. Well, after that heavy dose of one hour by Dr.D'Souza we had a lunch break. In the break the three of us went out to Rangoli and had pav bhaji. We met some other guys from our batch there. We interacted with them and then came back to college for our first dead body dissection class.

There was a tutorial class that was held before the real dissection. It was supposed to be a class where everyone was to be briefed about how to go forward with dissecting a human body. But the class rather turned out to be 'who is the bright one' kind of stuff. It was conducted by Mr.Manjrekar himself and all he did was throw questions at people about the human body. To me the questions sounded pretty easy but surprisingly to the rest of the class they seemed like bouncers bowled by Brett Lee. I guessed no one did read Cunningham's these days after all. As the class came to an end I had managed to answer around ten questions…well that's just me being modest. In fact I had nailed this class…I had an answer to every question that our HOD had for us. It had even lead him making a remark how he saw a huge potential in me and how he thought under right guidance I could be one of the best doctors this country would ever see. I guess since that day I became Mr.Manjrekar's favorite student. Anyway after the class got over we were given our roll numbers and assigned the tables for dissection. There is a very peculiar way in which the roll numbers in most of the schools and colleges in India are assigned. They are mostly according to surnames. So this in turn lead to Aman Sarin that is me being roll number 104 and Aisha Rahim being roll number 101. Each dissection table was to have fifteen people on it that meant Aisha and I were to be on the same table. Holy mother of god! I thought to myself, why things couldn't just go according to the plan.

A strong stench of formalin filled the dissection hall. The sight was horrifying. There were ten tables in a hall which had ten dead human bodies on them. The look of everything and the accompanying odor could make anyone who was not blind or suffering from sinusitis nauseous. I could see couple of girls throwing up and a few of them fainted. But to me all of this was more fascinating than disturbing. I had signed up to be a doctor after all and somewhere down my life I would be seeing surgeries on a living human so these blood drained cadavers preserved for more than three months hardly created any turmoil in my head. I went up to my table and waited patiently for the havoc to settle and begin with the proceedings.

'Well people throwing up and fainting…it's not how I imagined my first day of college to be. What about you?' I turned around to look where the voice had come from. It was Aisha who had taken her seat right opposite mine. I smiled back at her.

'For what I might say you made quite an impression in the demonstration room.' She continued.

'Well what can I say…I did not have the slightest idea that people these days didn't read Cunningham's…believe me if I had known that I would have burnt that book to ashes.' I said.

'Well it's good for you that you didn't burn it. It at least made you look like a big suck up.' Oh only god knew how much I wanted to come back at her with a sarcastic comment following that but what the hell she was beautiful. Somehow a meek shrug appealed more to me at that time.

'So Mr.Smarty Pants do you know the actual process of dissecting a human body because I can't wait to get started.' She asked.

'Yes as a matter of fact I do and just FYI the name is Aman.' Smarty pants...what the fuck was she thinking.

'Hey...it's Aisha' she said stretching her hand forward for a hand shake.

The rest of the day was pretty uneventful. We did dissect the cadaver and saw the pectoralis major muscle. Everyone at my table was really impressed by me because I played a major role in the dissection process. Aisha and I exchanged phone numbers and the first day in college finally came to an end.

Over the next couple of weeks it kept raining heavily. I was really enjoying myself in college. My popularity was growing steadily and soon I became that guy who knew it all and yet was not a complete geek. I developed a good relationship with all my friends and seniors. We used to go for dinner together every night and used to catch up on all movies that were released every weekend. Things between me and Aisha were going well. Both of us loved talking to each other and hanging around during college hours. We also had nice long phone calls that really made me believe that she was into me. I was also learning to play the six strings and Krish was turning out to be a great teacher.

The class elections for the class representative were going to be conducted and I found myself running for the post. I had a great campaign and all my friends really chipped in to make it a huge success. As a result I did win the election by a huge margin. It felt like I was living the dream that every guy who gets out of school and goes to college has. A considerable popularity amongst his peers, a fancy college in a mindblowing city, a great group of friends and to top it all a hot girlfriend. Well the girlfriend part wasn't true as of now but in Aisha I did have a possible candidate in the running.

In the last week of August the Fresher's Party was organized. It had finally stopped raining making the temperatures go up again marking the end to what had been one of the best monsoons in my life. The party was held at the multipurpose hall in the Dental College. The dress code was formals and I wore a purple Provogue shirt, black trousers, a black waist coat and a black tie for the occasion. Krish Madhur and I had arrived at the venue and were chatting up with a few other friends of ours. All the girls were wearing saris and somehow I was coming to terms with the fact that nothing makes a woman look more beautiful than a sari. This in turn made me really curious about how Aisha would look in a sari. My curiosity was soon laid to rest and was replaced with something that if I have to define would be a condition of pure awe as I saw her walk in through the entrance. She was wearing a black sari which made her look simply breath taking. The party went well. It mostly consisted of people from my batch being called up on the podium in pairs and the people from the batches senior to us made a complete mockery out of them. But it was all in good humor and all of us had a great time. I was awarded the Mr. Best Dressed Award. Madhur won Mr.Freshers Award. After the party got over I offered Aisha that I walk her back to her hostel and she agreed. We were walking through the campus towards her hostel…it was around nine at night and we basked in the moonlight which was the only source of light that illuminated the road.

'Did I tell you that you look amazing tonight?' I said.

'Ahhh…thank you Aman…that's really kind of you but this sari is really making me uncomfortable. And ya you look good too. Of course I don't have to tell you that…you have an award to show.' She said.

'Hmmm…you know something Aisha just wait here I have something that I left upstairs I'll be right back.'

I ran back to hall looking for Krish. I found him talking to Gurlyn. I asked him for his guitar which he said was kept at the Dj console. I grabbed the guitar and ran back down to Aisha. She looked a little surprised seeing the guitar in my hand.

'Is that your guitar?' she said

'No it's Krish's but I wanna play a song for you.' I said panting.

'Right now?'

'Well yes… is there a problem.'

'No…so what do you wanna play.' She asked

I picked up the guitar put the strap around my neck and strummed the C chord twice and broke into the song…it was Hero by Enrique Iglesias.

'*I can be your hero baby…I can kiss away your tears…I will stand by you forever…if you can take my breath away.'* As I finished the song and looked up at her she stood there stunned.

'That was amazing Aman…you never told me you played the guitar.' She finally spoke.

'Aisha this is not about me playing the guitar…if I didn't have a guitar and had a *tambora* instead I would still say what I'm about to say now. And it is that ever since I saw you I can't get you out of my head. The best part of every day that I live is the time I spend with you, talking to you, hanging around you, being with you. I really like you Aisha and I know despite the religious difference between us I wanna be with you. Will you go out with me?' As I said these words to her I felt vulnerable. It felt like I had exposed my jugular vein to her and I was praying that she doesn't turn out to be a vampire and go for the kill. But she did. Although she didn't grow long canines and come biting at me but she killed me softly with her words. She said that although she loved spending time with me and enjoyed my company she didn't have strong feelings towards me. She said she loved me as a friend. And because of the religious differences it would be really difficult for us to work out things. She said that she hoped all this wouldn't change how things were between us. And even though I said that things won't change, they did. That night I cried like a little baby. The nasty reality about rejection had smacked me in the face for the first time and I wasn't enjoying it one bit.

Over the next couple of days I and Aisha drew apart and our conversations were limited to mere greetings on the dissection table. I started bunking college more often as the sole reason for those six hours in college seeming worthwhile now seemed obsolete. To add insult to injury Aisha and Krish had become great friends. What started as a random conversation regarding me and how I was shattered over the incidence had developed into deep friendship. I guess Aisha felt lonely after I stopped talking to her and Krish and Gurlyn had a falling apart so they found refuge in each other's company. I did not appreciate Krish developing any kind of relationship with Aisha and felt betrayed under the terms of the BRO CODE, so I moved out of the room and got myself a single room on the ninth floor.

Two months down the line Krish and Aisha fell hopelessly in love with each other and started dating. It was then that I realized that I was being a total ass and all my actions were just unreasonable. I came to terms with the fact that Aisha was indeed the one that got away. But I still had a chance to get back that friendship that we had. I had a talk with Krish and Aisha and apologized for my behavior in the past few months. They really understood me and told me that they were worried about me a lot. I was glad that I was back on good terms with Krish and Aisha and was really happy for them. I guess some things in life are better understood the hard way, the real deal behind true friendship is one such thing. As for us, Krish, Aisha, Madhur and I went on to becoming best friends forever.

> *"Do you ever question your life…do you ever wonder why*
> *Do you ever see in your dreams…all the castles in the sky*
> *Oh tell me why…do we build castles in the sky*
> *Oh tell me why…all the castles pass us by."*
>
> —*Ian Van Dahl*

8
I GUESS THAT I'M HAUNTED TO BE WANTED

November 2008

It had been a long and tiring day and all I wanted to do was lay in bed listen to some good music and lull myself to sleep. My term exams were just around the corner and all I had been up to lately was passing my whole day in the library slogging it off. I guess eight hours of non-stop mugging can really get to a man. Well I don't know about others but it was really getting the best of me and at the end of the day all that I really wanted was my fair share of rest. I had finished my dinner and had excused myself from the guys who were in Madhur's room watching *The Dark Knight* to get some much needed sleep. It was 11.40 at night and I was lying down on my bed while listening to some music on my phone. The music was all I could hear and the rest of the world had just seemed as if it had dissolved in the vicinity. Nothing else did exist at that moment. It was just me, the darkness in the room and a feeling of vast emptiness which made the feeling amazing. Emptiness, it does sound like a very disappointing word doesn't it? But I guess when there is so much going on in your life that you hardly have time to breathe emptiness sure does come like a boon in disguise. I guess Enigma was somehow responsible for it. I love Enigma, the music was nothing but divine. But the lyrics I don't have a clue what they mean. Somehow those empty thoughts with those empty words of Enigma took me into a state of trance. It felt like I was living in a parallel universe where my life wasn't a rat race. A sudden vibration of my phone and the song abruptly coming to an end brought me back to reality. I checked out my phone to find out it was a reminder. The date was 23rd November. It was a reminder I had set over two years back. It was a reminder that today was mine and Aarti's anniversary.

It had been over four 4 months since Aarti had passed away and seven months since I had moved on with my life following our break up. Although I was chemically programmed to feel sad and depressed there was some chemical *locha* in me that had not allowed Aarti's death to leave a significant impact on my life. Even though flashes of her and the times I spent with her still haunted me I somehow had found an escape route in Mumbai and everything here. I had started a new life in a new place with new people who knew nothing about me. They had no idea of my past and what I had been through. Sometimes it is really nice to live in a place and among people who don't know you. It really makes you start all over again. And what a start I had made. Sure there were a few hiccups like the ones with Aisha and Krish. But all in all I was happy to get away from those deserted roads of Nagpur where I and Aarti used to go for our long drives. I was happy to be in a city of skyscrapers where you didn't have a comfortable house of your own. Getting away from those deer parks where I had shared my first kiss with her really made me happy. Everything in Nagpur, every road, every coffee house, and every garden had some or the other memory of Aarti imprinted on it. So yes I was really happy to put all that behind me and come and live in Mumbai. It was like this entire city was a blank canvas for me and I could draw out my life any way I wanted and let the colors thrill me.

But then no matter where you go and what you do there is no running away from yourself.., there is no running away from your past, there is no running away from memories and there is no running away from life. That is of course not true if you have Alzimer's which is something I don't have so it all held true for me. I was so madly in love with her that letting her go so easy wasn't going to be easy at all. No matter how much I tried to avoid the thought of Aarti I always knew that she would come back to haunt me. That girl did not allow me to live in peace when she was alive so it was certainly too much to ask for when she was resting in peace and had all the time in the world to bring that love lost feeling back into my life. The process had begun and the sands of time were storming by. Time had started taking a backward flow. And when it stopped I found myself standing at this very day two years ago.

As I have told you already that I had lived all my life in Nagpur and had gone to the same school for fifteen years. Aarti had come to study at my school from sixth grade. And it was back then itself that I had fallen head over heels for her. Things had turned out very well for us and we had eventually become best pals. So after knowing her for over four years I had realized that I was deeply in love with her and had decided to ask her out. Over the years that had passed a girl and a guy going out was no longer considered a taboo. And in 2006 a guy was considered uncool if he did not have more than a 100 friends and 200 scraps on ORKUT. And he was a homo if he hadn't gone out with a girl, if only for one night. Such public norms did not bother me because I had a reputation that spoke volumes about me. Chances of the guys in my school one day getting up and calling me a homo were equal to the chances of seeing a dinosaur while walking in Manhattan. It was love and only immense love for Aarti that had made me come to this decision.

On 22nd November 2006 at 9.30 PM I was alone in my house as my parents had gone away for a couple of days to attend some relative's wedding in Mount Abu. I was watching television when her text came. It was one of those SMS jokes that people forward. I really hated the entire custom of forwarding SMS to a bunch of people. Personally I thought it was just a way in which people told you 'Hey forgotten me? I am still alive.' I replied back with another one of those jokes. Two minutes later she sent me another one which was indeed very funny and had me in splits. I replied with a LOL. And there after the series of texting began which lasted for two hours. I guess we must have exchanged fifty texts between us and I swear to god most of them were just psychobabble. Finally her text came which said that her parents had fallen asleep and I could call her if I wanted. It was a golden opportunity for me. I could ask her out over the phone. The phone has always been my loyal friend. I am good with words so the phone always makes me sound good. I could baffle anyone over the phone with my bullshit and they would still buy it. It also gives me a royal option of listening to whatever I want to and ignoring what I want to. In such situation I think my favorite person is Alexander Grahame Bell. If I had to do this all in person looking face to face with another human I would be nothing but a guy with sweaty palms and shivering legs uttering some shit in a stammer. I thanked god that he was saving me of such humiliation because no matter what…I was going to tell Aarti that I loved her and that mixed emotion of anxiety and fear could not stop me.

The phone call went very well. We talked about school and friends and songs and movies. The conversation then shifted to crushes and I had a break through. I told her that ever since I had first seen her I could never get enough of her. Every day I left her in school or college but the thought of being with her never evaded me. I told her that I loved her from the bottom of my heart and can't imagine living a life of which she was not a part of. She told me that she felt the same way and I think my heart literally skipped a beat. I sang for her…song after song. It was when I was singing *O meri Jaan* from Life in a Metro that she started crying. She said that she had never felt this way about anyone and that everything seemed very scary. She asked me never to go away from her life as she could not live if I broke her heart. It was just one of those moments again that make me wanna cry. I tried hard not to but then I was overflowing with emotions that I could not hold back any longer. I cried and she cried and in between those soft sobbing voices we kept telling each other that we loved each other and no matter what happens we will be together for the rest of our lives. It was finally 6 AM in the morning when we reluctantly hung up on each other. I had pulled off my first all-nighter which was just the beginning of many more to come. I still remember that night because I had pulled off a conversation with Aarti for almost nine hours.

The whirlpool of memories drowned me further into the thoughts of Aarti. I found myself in the setting of my first kiss. The time was around six in the evening and the sky was dimly lit up by the fading rays of the setting sun. The birds were flying back home. We were in the deer park on Seminary hills. There were lush green trees all around us and hundreds of deers in their cage. A toy train goes around Seminary hills which circles around that deer park. There is a rickety slide next to the train track. We were sitting on the steps of that slide. She was sitting on a step that was above mine. We sat there hand in hand looking mindlessly at those deer. It felt as if we had locked our entire world in a box somewhere and had run away to be with each other amongst those innocent creatures. That park was our favorite hangout spot. We would just bunk tuitions and come here and sit. We did not talk much. We just sat hand in hand and looked at those deer and into each other eyes. What did matter was being with each other and feeling the same way about each other till the sun went down and the park closed down. That day was no different. I was just loving being with her with her hand in my hand as I left all my thoughts behind me and lived that moment. I turned my head to look at her and caught her staring at me. Our eyes met and I got lost in them. She always had watery eyes I don't know whether it was a medical condition or what but they reminded me of the eyes of a cute Labrador. They have so much innocence in them and they look at you and you think that they are going to cry any moment…it so makes you feel like hugging her tightly and telling that everything is going to be alright. Well that is what I wanted to do. I wanted to hug Aarti and tell her that even if the world crashes down over me I would never leave her. I had completely lost track of time. I hadn't noticed the black clouds that had covered the sky. And then it started raining and I kept looking at her, into her eyes, as we got wet sitting on that slide. We were drenched and it was pouring heavily but I did not want to kill this moment which felt surreal. I moved my hand towards her and gently pushed aside that strand of hair back over her ear. My hand moved down and forward to cup her left cheek. I leaned forward still looking into her eyes and she shut them close. I left a kiss on her forehead her left eye and the tip of her nose and retreated. She slowly opened her eyes and looked into my eyes and then at my lips. She then leaned forward and stopped almost inches away from my face. I could sense her deep slow breath over my neck. Then she closed her eyes again and spelled it out for me…KISS ME. I covered the last few inches which was the distance that was separating us. I closed my eyes as our lips met and all of us sudden I was in a world of blind ecstasy. All that prevailed were senses. The feel of her hand playing with my hair…the feel of the rain and my wet t- shirt on my skin…the sweet smell of wet soil…the feel of her breath on my face…and the best of all was the feeling of her soft lips on mine…it all felt magical. I never knew that such a feeling existed. For the first time in my life I was experiencing pleasure like I had never felt before even with my eyes open. When we finally broke the kiss I felt love like I had never felt before. I hugged Aarti and told her that I loved her a lot and she was the most beautiful thing that had ever happened to me.

I was still swimming in the ocean of all the memories that I had of Aarti. It was all coming back to me now. *Kabhi Alvida Naa Kehna*…the first movie that we had seen together…those n- number of songs that I had sung for her…all the coffees that we shared together…all the bike rides that we took. The list was just endless. The first time we slept together was another memory that stood out. Although it was not a great memory because it was very lousy…neither of us knew what to do and when it did finally happen the right way I climaxed within minutes…yet it was a memory that was very close to me…We had lost our virginity after all. It finally ended with the memory of our break up and that phone call from her that I had received on my radio show saying that she wanted me back in her life. Thinking about all this and knowing that the person who had made my life a blissful dream didn't exist anymore made me feel pathetic. I wanted to tell Aarti that everything was alright. I wanted to tell her that we could be together again. I wanted to tell her that all this moving on with my life business was an act and I still felt the same way about her. But I couldn't tell her. There was nothing I could do. I had never felt so helpless in my entire life. There was nothing I could do…not a single thing could get her back. And then the last words that Aarti had said to me clouded every other thought. 'It is better to let go of someone who loves you…than keeping him… in love with you, when you know you just can't be with him.' That is what she had said. At that time those words didn't seem to make

57

any sense. At that time they didn't help me get out of my misery. My heart felt heavy as the thought of Aarti's death had finally sunk in. Tears felt like cinder and as I cried it felt like my eyes were spitting fire. I was angry at myself for being a complete asshole. I felt as if it was entirely my fault. I needed someone who could comfort me…someone who could tell me that it's not my fault. I decided that I was going to go and tell Krish and Madhur about it. Over the time we had all become really close so I saw no point withholding secrets from them. And plus Krish was a genius at making people feel better and he understood me better than anyone else in the world. So I went to see them both.

I found them in Madhur's room. Krish was on the phone talking to Aisha and Madhur who had finished watching *The Dark Knight* was now hooked on to his laptop again and was watching *House MD*. I told them that I wanted to talk to them about something important and within no time Krish hung up on Aisha and Madhur switched off their laptops…and were all ears. I narrated my story to them. I sobbed during the whole narration. They heard all of it intently.

'Dude I think you should sleep it off.' Krish said. 'You have been very brave following everything that has happened and I am sure when you wake up tomorrow it won't hurt as much.'

'I can't fucking sleep dude…when I lay down on my bed in the emptiness of my room those fucking thoughts become even more profound.' I said disappointed that the guy in whom I had a lot of faith couldn't come up with a better solution.

'You can sleep in my room…just get your mattress and sleep here.

We will watch *House* or may be a movie and it will distract you.' Madhur chipped in with another sucky but still better solution.

'Or you could do something that works best in such conditions.' Krish said.

'What?' I asked him.

'Naa...on second thought forget it...plus you would never be up for it.' Krish's words were getting me all curious.

'Just tell me what the fuck it is man.' I said getting impatient.

'You could get drunk...and by drunk I mean totally sloshed so that there is no room for thoughts in your head.' And the man was back...Bravo Krish Bravo.

'Ya...that sounds great.' I said.

'But dude mind you...you have to get sloshed as in complete *talli*...or else you would just end up feeling more vulnerable. And I and Madhur will be the judges of whether you are drunk enough or not. If you agree to this then only we will go or else forget it' Krish was not kidding about this.

'Okay...what the hell...let's do this' I said

So we were off for our first *daroo* party. It was 2.30 AM and we went to the only place where we could get liquor at this hour...Hotel Sunrise. It was a C grade hotel in a dingy shady alley next to the Thane Belapur Highway. I had heard that all kinds of stuff happened in there. Prostitution...Hooka...Drinks...Drugs...if you needed anything once the moon was out you go to Hotel Sunrise. There was even a famous motto all around Nerul which was...In Hotel Sunrise it is never late until sunrise. Well anyway we went up to the restaurant on the first floor and ordered a round of beers. I had tasted beer earlier so it went down well. It was Kingfisher Mild my favorite beer. Then we ordered another round…then another…and another. I was feeling it now. I could feel my inhibitions wearing off and the even the Tacky music being played sounded fantastic. I began dancing around in the restaurant and was joined by a few other people who were as drunk as me or maybe even more as they kept stumbling. Well now I knew why all those songs like *Beedi jaliele* and *Billo rani* become so famous. When you get drunk such *chichore* songs make you dance. I was dancing…well I guess in that state of mind I could have even danced to the sound of a generator. Yes I was drunk…but not drunk enough. Krish offered me a cigarette…I didn't want to accept it. But he told me that smoking with alcohol heightens the high. So I took that Cancer Stick from him and lit it. Till this day I regret that decision. It was the first time I kissed the butt of a cigarette and I have not been able to kick it since. I ordered another beer and another. It took eight pints of beer and five cigarettes to knock me out. After that I only had a faint memory of what happened. There are flashes that I remember of stumbling across the road with Krish and Madhur supporting me and of me throwing up on the sidewalks.

That night didn't actually solve the purpose for which it was intended. Sure it worked wonders that night but even now the thought of Aarti hasn't completely evaded me. It sure is a lot less painful now as I have cleared my conscious that I was in no way responsible for Aarti's death and that her death was nothing but an unfortunate accident. But the subconscious is beyond my control. Still at times when I sit idle all by myself a thought always crosses my mind that perhaps things could have worked out differently. Perhaps if I would have called her I wouldn't feel so guilty after all. Perhaps we still would have been together. If she would have called me the day I was flying to Mumbai then perhaps she would be alive. Perhaps...Perhaps...Perhaps. But there is nothing that you can do about all the 'PERHAPS's'. Life still moves on and we move on with it. Her words now make a whole lot more sense. 'It is better to let go of someone who loves you...than keeping him... in love with you, when you know you just can't be with him' is what she had said and I guess it's all true. But still sometimes when I am lying on my bed all alone at night and I stare into that empty darkness...a thought crosses my mind...If only god gave me a chance to change one thing in my life...then *perhaps* things would have worked out differently.

9
SHE IS THE ONE...I THINK

December 2008

The winter breaks were on and it was the first time I had come back home since college started. The month was December and New Year was just around the corner. Nagpur is just one of those cities where one can enjoy every season to its maximum. The temperatures go soaring high in summers. But the plight of the people is laid to rest by the rains. And then there are winters. The mercury drops by this time to five to six degrees and it really gets cold. I had been here for five days now and all these days I had done nothing but watch movies in my room and laze around in my blanket. Believe me there is nothing better than getting cozy in your blanket on a winter morning in Nagpur.

I had no friends left here. All my best friends had taken admissions somewhere else. Most of them were in Pune, some in Delhi and the rest were just somewhere else. So as I was telling you I was on a

movie watching marathon. For some odd reason I was watching all
the romantic comedies that have ever been made. I started with 'When
Harry Met Sally' then 'Sleepless in Seattle' then 'You've got Mail'
and by the time I was done watching 'French Kiss' I was in love with
Meg Ryan. I was in my bedroom listening to some music. Well for
some odd reason I remember the very song that was playing at that
time. It was 'I don't wanna miss a thing by Aerosmith'. That is the
time I got this phone call. It was Riya.

'hello.'

'hi Aman! Its Riya.'

'oh hi Riya! How are you? Long time.'

'yes it's been long. I'm doing well. How have you been?'

'I have been good. Have just come back home for the winters.'

'ya I saw that as your facebook status. So that's why I thought I'll
catch up with you.

'oh that's great. It's great that you called. I have been in Nagpur for
five days now and I'm getting really bored.'

'oh! why is that? What's happening?'

'Nothing re. Don't really have any friends left in town so kinda
haven't been out. And plus mom dad left for a short vacation to Fiji
so I'm here all by myself with my dog.'

'That is sad. By the way why didn't you call me then? Am I not
your friend?'

'No Riya don't take it that way. It didn't come to me that you are
here. I mean it's been so long since I saw you last. It really didn't
occur to me.'

'hmmm. Don't worry Mr.Aman I will be your savior and free you of your boredom.'

'Well that's very kind of you.'

'So tell me when are you going back to Bombay?'

'I am due to go back day after tomorrow.'

'Oye you just came. Why so soon ?'

' Arre we medical people don't get too many holidays. And plus no one is going to be home too so that's why.'

'Okay so we really don't have much time on hand. You should have called me earlier na.'

'Sorry yaar I don't know what to say.'

'Okay forget the sorry worry. Tell me what time can you meet me?'

'You want to meet today?'

'Why is there a problem?'

'No, no problem. How about 1730 hours?'

'1730 hours!! What the fuck dude? Are you sure you are doing medicine? That sounds like you work for the army or something.'

'Well it's a long story will tell you once I meet you. Yes so is 5.30 in the evening okay?'

'Yes 5.30 sounds great.'

'So what place?'

'We will decide it ya. You come pick me up first.'

'I have to pick you up?'

'Duh uh don't you know you have to pick up your dates. What is the matter with you?'

'Well I have been single for quite some time now I guess the rules of dating have changed.'

'That makes you sound really old.'

'Ha! Well I'm older than you at least.'

'HA HA very funny. Now stop cracking stupid jokes and take down my address.'

Now I so didn't understand what the joke was and what was funny. I wasn't even trying to be funny. But then I didn't mention anything and took down her address.

'Okay so I'll pick you up at 5.30'

'Ya okay I'll see you then. And please don't be late.'

'No I won't .'

So we hung up. Finally after five days in Nagpur I was going to get out of my house. And I was going on a date with Riya. The whole thought was very amusing. I was excited about it. I had my lunch. I had a bath and got ready. I had a real hard time selecting what to wear. I know the whole thing about selecting what to wear sounds all girly and all. But it was my first date with this girl. I had to look my very best. It had been a long time since Aarti happened. And now I thought I finally needed some closure and had to move on. So after about half an hour of trying on different clothes I finally decided to go with the blue jeans and a white shirt. I wore my Davidoff Cool Water which is my favorite perfume and I was good to go.

I pulled up my car outside Riya's building at 5.25 and called her to tell her that I had arrived. She said she would be down in 5 minutes.

And in another 5 minutes she came down. She was wearing a green top and black three fourths. As she was walking from her gate to the car all I could think was how fabulous she looked. I swear to god at that moment I even thought she was more beautiful than Catherine Zeta Jones. I got out of my car and pulled the door open for her.

'Gosh! You are looking drop dead gorgeous.'

'Gee thanks Aman.'

'Oh don't mention it. It's my honor to be on a date with someone as wonderful as you.'

'Oh please cut it out. Now you're just making me blush.'

'Okay fine. So tell me where do you wanna go?'

'Well I don't know. Where do you wanna go?'

'Hey I'm cool with anything. I insist you pick the place. *Waise bhi* I haven't been here in like five months so I don't really know about any new places.'

'Well I am not hungry right now so I guess we'll just go for a drive if that's fine by you.'

'Okie Tokie.'

So I began driving around Civil Lines and then towards the Telangkhedi lake which is like one of my favorite places in Nagpur. It's this huge public lake which is crowded with people in the evening where loads of roadside hawkers sell bhutta especially in June and July. A lot of couples come and sit on the parapet of the lake. Just spend time with each other. Look at the sun setting in the far horizon. I have never been a big fan of such places where couples come and hang out. There are those shady corners in which if you look you will be like 'oh god I will get you a room.' So ya this is just one of those places. But then there is this other end of the lake where no one goes. It's not developed. It has this patch of grass that leads to the lake. That is the place where you can go and sit and feel in a whole different place altogether far away from the hustle bustle of the city. But the real reason why I really love this place is for the road around it. It is the road leading up to Vayu Sena Nagar and Seminary hills. It's got a lot of gardens and open meadows around it and then there is this patch that makes you feel like you are driving through a forest. That road has also got a deer park which I remember because of the times I spent with Aarti there. I guess it was in that very park that I had my first kiss in the rains.

Anyway I was driving on that road now and although all the memories of the time I spent with Aarti were flashing me by I was on a date with this lovely girl whose company I was really enjoying. Then as if she had read my mind Riya started talking about Aarti.

'By the way I am really sorry about Aarti.'

'Oh ya so am I.'

'I mean I really wanted to call you and check out on how you were doing after I heard but I guessed you didn't wanna talk about it.'

'Ya I know it was a shocker.'

'So are you over her now?'

'Well yes sure. It's been what five, six months since that happened and it is not as if we were still seeing each other.'

'That is kind of cold on your behalf. I mean you had been dating her for like two years. Everyone in school looked up to you as the perfect couple. She certainly had to mean more to you than that.'

'Oh come on Riya. What do you want me to say? I was all depressed and lonely. My heart was shattered to pieces. I couldn't sleep at night. That the thought of me talking to her one day and the next day she just goes away forever horrified me. Is that want you want to hear? If that is so then I'm sorry to disappoint you Riya but I certainly didn't feel any of it. I'm sorry that things didn't work out the way people wanted them to be.'

'Hey relax. Sorry to spoil your mood. I know you have been through a lot.'

'No dammit I have not been through a lot. I'm not a pity puppet for god sake. I do not need your sympathies. What I have been through is a great start to a new life. Amazing five months in college. I found a new place where I have made some great friends and have started a new life; a life of which Aarti is not a part of.'

'Ok fine! So anyway tell me if you are dating someone currently in college.'

'What the hell is wrong with you? My girlfriend just died a few months ago.'

'Ummmmmm'

'How could you even ask me that?'

'Ummmmmmm.'

'Hey chill I'm just kidding with you. What! You never get sarcasm?'

'It's not funny Aman. It really is not funny. You seriously scared the hell out of me.'

'Oh come on. It's better than you torturing me with all that Aarti stuff. And no I am not seeing anyone in college as of now.'

'Ok. Why no hot girls in college?'

'Well there are a few but none of them has really seemed interesting enough.'

'Hmmmm.'

'What about you? Are you seeing anyone?'

'Oh no I am as single as the last time you met me.'

'Well that's good for me I guess.'

'Huh! What?'

'It's like I can openly flirt with you and there won't be a possessive boyfriend running behind me to kick my ass.'

'Haha. God Aman you haven't changed a bit. You're the same old jolly fellow who knew how to put a smile on everyone's face with those comments. Ever since you passed out, school assembly hasn't been fun at all. Sure there is Raghav who is trying to fill your shoes with his retarded humor but you were just you. Everyone in school just loved you.'

'Oh you are just being kind. Anyway I can drive you around for hours but that way we will just be wasting fuel. How about we go get some coffee or something?'

'Fine.'

So we drove over to the Café Coffee Day in the VCA stadium to get some coffee and grab a bite. Riya ordered for an apple soda and I ordered a Tropical Iceberg which is something that I usually order at CCD. After the order came we got back to talking. We talked about my college, life in Mumbai, her life, school days friends, random people, movies, music, relationships and a lot of other things. Strangely I was finding myself get very comfortable with her. It was as if we had this connection which was making talking to her about things very easy. Sure I had known that she existed for like three years now and we were in the same school for fourteen years but I never knew her personally. I always thought of her as that girl who was dating this guy Palak. But now that I was getting to know her in person I really felt good about her. At that moment I could tell her anything I wanted to. I could answer any question she had for me. Was I falling for her? I did always think that she was hot and all but I think a lot of people are hot. I think one of my anatomy teachers is hot. But it's not every day that I go around talking to people I don't really know about my life. I guess I was falling for her. Oh God! I was falling for her. What was I to do? Was I supposed to tell her how I felt? Was I to ask her out? But that would lead to us being in a long distance thing. They certainly don't work out. I think all I needed was another date with her and a night to think about it. But the next day was New Year's Eve. She certainly must be having plans. And I was flying back to Mumbai on 1st Jan. Yet I gave it a shot.

'So tell me what your plans are for tomorrow? I mean New Year's.'

'Well I think I will be going out for this party at the Gondwana Club with my family'

'Oh that's good.'

'Why what are your plans?'

'No plans as of now. I might rent a movie or go visit my grandparents. I was wondering if you have some time we could meet up tomorrow too. Anyway I'm flying back to Mumbai on 1st.'

'Ya sure I would love to meet up tomorrow. *Waise bhi* I'll be going to the party at 10 or 10.30 at night so we can meet up the same time as today.'

'Fine then it's a date.'

'It sure is.'

After a lot of arguing about who pays the bill with her being insistent on splitting it, we split it. It was 20:00 hours when I finally dropped her off at her place. The two and half hours I had spent with her just seemed like two and a half minutes. Time does fly by quickly when you are doing something you really like. It's just like watching a movie that you really like or reading a book you are really enjoying. Bloody you never figure out how much time it has been till it's finally over. As she gave me a peck on my cheek told me she had a lovely time I felt like holding her in my arms and kissing her straight away. As she got out of the car and started walking towards her colony gate I felt that this is one girl I really want to be with forever. Suddenly that one night to think about it and the long distance thing didn't seem to matter. I waited till her figure disappeared into the far end through her colony gate and then started my car and drove back home. I had figured out that I was going to ask Riya out tomorrow. Now all I had to do was to ask her out in a way she couldn't refuse.

10
FOOL PROOF PLAN

New Year's Eve 2008-2009

I got up today with a strange feeling building within me. I was erupting with enthusiasm yet something was asking me to take it easy. I was filled with joy and the whole thought made me smile. Yet something about it got me scared to the point that I even thought of dropping the whole idea. There was a storm raging in my head. It was throwing at me different techniques that I could imply to make the plan work. Something told me that I should go on with it because I was superb with this. But then something told me *'bhai tu toh gaand pe laat kha ke hi maanega.'* Finally after talking to myself, arguing with myself, consoling myself, getting pissed off at myself, I gathered the courage to go ahead and execute the plan. The plan was simple. I had to ask out Riya. But after yesterday I had realized something which led to the revision of the plan. The current plan was – I had to ask out Riya in a way that she wouldn't say no. How easy did it sound? It was like telling a lion to go fetch its prey. As easy as it looks only the lion knows what goes into catching a deer.

Lots of ideas for the perfect date had crossed my mind. There was just one problem with all of them. Each one of them had a flaw.

1)   Taking her out for a lovely movie say *Jab We Met.*

Flaw – Movie seriously…who asks a girl out on a movie date?

2)   Renting a good movie and watching it together.

Flaw – Can't I think beyond movies.

3)   How about a horror movie. She will get scared and hold me tight.

Flaw – seriously cut it out.

4)   Dinner in a romantic restaurant.

Flaw – Dinner at 5.30 PM? Are you fucking out of your mind.

5)   Long drive to Fun and Food village.

Flaw – *Abe date pe ja raha hai ya picnic manane ja raha hai?*

6)   Candle light dinner….oh sorry supper on the school terrace.

Flaw – *Ha jaroor. School toh tere dada ki property hai na.*

7)   Taking her to the mall.

Flaw – *Nagpur ke malls*…do I even have to say it. ok they suck!!!

They kept flowing in and breezing out one after the other. Just as I had set up my mind on the long drive bit and had gone to the terrace to get a quick smoke, the perfect idea struck me. Mom and Dad were out of town so I had the house to myself. The terrace of my house is a great place. It is surrounded by trees on all sides so it gives a great secluded getaway place without drawing the attention of the pesky neighbors. Being the huge music buff that I am I had a great collection of songs to set the mood right. And as the day is shorter in winters the sun would set by 6 PM and it would give me a great opportunity for a candlelight supper arrangement. The equation fitted perfectly.

Home Terrace = Nice Place

Great Music = Good Mood

Candlelight supper = Romantic setting

And when you add Nice Place + Good Mood + Romantic Setting it sums up to a Perfect Date.

Now there were just two other things that would make this mastermind plan fool proof. First, the place needed some decoration and furniture placement. Second, I needed some good luck coming my way. Well there is nothing that I could do about the second thing so I decided to leave it to god and work on the first thing. I got the plastic table from the kitchen and placed it right in the center of the terrace. Then I got two chairs and placed them on the two opposite sides of the table. Finally I got a nice white table cloth and put it on the table. It was now time for the decorations so I went to the market close by. I picked up some scented candles and some balloons, mainly heart shaped red balloons. Then I went to the florist and picked up fifty red and fifty white roses. I did pick up something else but for now I guess I will keep it a secret.

It took me around two hours to decorate the place. By the time I was done it was 3PM. I called up Riya.

'Hey Riya! Whats up?'

'Nothing much re just had lunch. You tell me what's up with you?'

'Actually I was just calling to confirm our date this evening. Are we still on for 5.30?'

'Obviously we are. Why do you have other plans?'

'Oh! No, no other plans just confirming.'

'Well I don't care even if you did. You would anyway have to cancel them.'

'*Arre* no ya. No other plans I just wanna take you out for a very special date tonight.'

'*O accha!* What do you have in mind?'

'You will have to wait for that.'

'Fine then. Pick me up at 5.30.'

'Okie Tokie.'

So it was on. It was going to happen. Aman Sarin was going to ask out Riya Mathur. I had a bath and got ready. Today I didn't care about the way I looked. Today I did not spend half an hour figuring out what clothes to wear. Today I did not spend my time in front of the mirror trying out weird hair do's. Today I spent my time waiting. Waiting for that clock to strike five. And when it was finally 5.10, I was on my way to pick Riya up.

I pulled up my car outside Riya's colony at 5.20. I called her up. She said she would be right down. Then I called Domino's and ordered a large pepperoni pizza and a large bottle of coke and asked them to deliver it to my place. At 5.27 I saw Riya walking towards me from her colony gate. And once again that feeling took over me. It felt like she was bringing a fresh breath of air in my life. I felt my heart beating rapidly in my chest. It looked as if she gave me a reason to be a better man.

'*Oye hero yahi baithna hai ki kahi chalna bhi hai?*'

She snapped me out of my day dream.

'Oh ya lets go.'

I started driving.

'So where are we going?'

'Home.'

'*Arre par abhi toh date suru hui hai.* Don't you wanna woo me first or at least get me drunk before we make out?'

'Well as great as that sounds I think will pass on that today. Maybe some other time.'

'Then why are we going home? Let's go someplace else na.'

'No we are going home. And you shall see what great plans I have for today.'

'Okay'

So we reached home at 5.40. I lead her into my house and got her to sit on the sofa in the living room.

'So, what now?' She said.

'You look absolutely mind blowing.' I replied.

'See, I knew you were going to woo me with your charm and make out with me.'

'Oh did you? So now what? Are you going to resist it or allow me to woo you.' I said and moved closer to her.

'Well that depends.'

'Depends on what?'

'On how drunk you get me.'

'What if I intoxicated you with my words and get you started with my touch.' I was looking her straight in the eye now. I could feel her warm fast breath on my neck. I cupped her face with my hands and leaned in closer when the doorbell rang. I let her go and got up on my feet to see who it was.

'Cheap shot Aman. Cheap Shot.' I think there was some sort of rage building within her. This was clearly not a good sign. I cursed myself for getting carried away. It was 6.10 and the Domino's delivery had arrived.

'Sorry for the late delivery sir. My tyre got punctured. Had to walk back to the store and get a new bike. And as I didn't deliver in 30 minutes your Pizza is free.'

'Thank you.'

I closed the door as the guy handed me the Pizza and left. I looked at the sky and grabbed down a fistful from it. Domino's is never late. Except for today. I got a free pizza. I never get anything free. Even those scratch cards always read 'sorry better luck next time.' I guess we were back on track. I think good luck was just flowing in. The tide was changing. I decided to stick with the plan.

'So this is your idea of a great date? A Domino's pizza and making out.' She said still seeming angry.

'Hey come on. We were both in the moment and I got a bit carried away. Sorry for that. You wait I will get the pizza served.' And I left the room.

I came back after a few minutes.

'Food is served.'

I lead her up the stairs and onto the terrace. Neither of us spoke a word. Finally when we reached the terrace this is what we walked into. The terrace floor was covered with rose petals red and white. There were loose blown heart shaped balloons scattered all over the floor. There were roses cello taped to the table, chair and almost everything that was there. The table had two plates with a slice of pizza on them. There were two wine glasses filled to the brim with coke. There was soft music playing and the song was 'Wonderful tonight by Eric Clapton.' And the entire terrace was lit up with 10 scented candles tactfully placed in the right places. The expression on her face was priceless. She just stood there. She did not move, did not say a word. She just stood there with her hands over her open mouth. Finally she spoke.

'Aman why? Why did you have to do this?'

'I said I wanted to do something special for you. That's why.'

'This is truly special. It's more than special. It's just…amazing.'

'I know right.'

'So this is why we came home. It was not because you wanted to make out.'

'Hey I told ya. That too is a very alluring plan but not today. So should we eat or what.'

I sat her down on her chair and I took mine and we began eating. All of a sudden I heard her sobbing.

'Hey what's wrong?'

'Nothing.'

'Oh come on. *Bin matlab ke koi rota hai kya.*'

And then it came. She started weeping. I was feeling pretty weird. I mean firstly I put so much effort into planning this out and what does she do – cry.

'You must be thinking I'm really weird na?'

'No, not as yet. But I guess a little explanation would help me improve in the future.'

'It's not that Aman. All this is really beautiful. It's just that no one has ever done something like this for me before. And I feel bad about saying all those things to you before.'

'Hey come on. It's alright. Shit happens. You are a wonderful girl and for you I can do this every day.'

'Aman….'

I thought this was my best chance and I got down on one knee and pulled out that secret thing that I had brought from my pocket. It was a Plastic Red rose which was actually a case. I opened the case and there was a ring inside.

'Riya Mathur. Will you go out with me?'

Through her teary face a laugh escaped her mouth. 'Yes.'

'I love you Riya.'

'I love you too Aman.'

And we hugged. She hugged me so tightly I thought I would run out of breath. It felt amazing. After about two minutes we looked into each other's eyes. She had some tears rolling down her cheek. I kissed them. She held my head and kissed me on my lips. It was a hard passionate kiss. Her tongue moving in and out of my mouth. Our tongues twirling with each other. I nibbled on her lips and she bit mine. Our breathing grew faster. And rest as they say is history.

We had our food. We talked about us. About how we would go to any length to make this relationship work. How we would never let distance play a factor in separating us. We pledged unconditional love for each other. And then we made out some more in my room. I drove her back home at 9 PM. She gave me a good night kiss this time on the lips and departed. I felt like the world didn't matter. I felt like she completed me. It felt like life had become worth living.

She called me at 11.57 PM and we talked for a while. At midnight we wished each other a Happy New Year which marked the beginning of us as a couple. I also got a call from Mom and Dad. They did sound very happy in Fiji. My friends from college Krish, Madhur and Aisha also called to wish me. All of them were flying back to Mumbai tomorrow itself like I was. So I was going to see them in less than twenty four hours.

I got up the next morning at 7 AM and got packed and ready to leave for the airport. My driver drove me to the airport. My flight was on time and after getting checked in and doing the other needful I boarded the plane. Before takeoff I called Riya. She was really sleepy and sounded really dazed. I remember that day I said something to her that after that day I have never told her again. Maybe because my actions always said it for me. I said 'Babe I love you and I will love you till the last breath I breathe because Babe you take my breath away.' I don't think she really understood the depth of my words then. I think she doesn't even remember that I said something like that. You can't blame her though. It was just the sleep.

11

IS THIS WHAT HEAVEN FEELS LIKE?

January 2009, Mumbai

It had been a rather uneventful day. I had woken up in the same way like I do on rest of the days…that is… late in the afternoon with sleep in my eyes, a yawn on my mouth and a tent in my shorts. I had bathed and had ordered a pizza from Domino's. Done nothing but laze around in my room watching movie after movie. It was a day that my mother would definitely not term productive. Ever since I had got back from Nagpur my life had come down and become seriously unproductive. I would get up late, have a late lunch, either laze around in my room watching all the movies ever made by man or go to FAST MINDZ and play DOTA with the guys. FAST MINDZ was a gaming internet café situated in Sector 17 Nerul. Most of the guys who came there were gaming freaks and Krish Madhur and me were just turning into ones ourselves.

I swear I can write this whole book on DOTA if I want. It has got so many things that if I sit down to describe it for the people who haven't played it or heard of it my book would be as big as The Lord of the Rings. DOTA had become an integral part of my life and life without at least two hours of DOTA everyday was unimaginable...and secondly because if you have a person close to you who does play this highly addictive game then you must know the basics or you will be conveniently ignored from most of the conversations he involves in and believe me most of them will be about DOTA. I swear it's true. I know a guy who is 30 years old...is married...has a wife and two kids...has a job...he comes to FAST MINDZ and ignores his job and family day in and day out over that game. If he gets a call from his wife when he is playing he just lies through his teeth saying that he is in a meeting and will be late so she shouldn't wait up. Another guy I know broke up with his girlfriend when she asked him to make a choice between her and DOTA. Such is the love that players develop towards the game...so that's why I advise everyone who knows a DOTA player personally to at least know these basics about the Game.

Well my DOTA sessions would generally end late at night which led to having a late dinner somewhere post 10 o clock. Term exams had gotten over in November itself and we had time until late April for our University exams. At night the guys would hang out at my room and we would watch some TV series mostly *House* and discuss various DOTA strategies. Somewhere past midnight Riya called and we would spend a good half an hour talking to each other. It wasn't even a month that we had started seeing each other and we loved what they say is the honeymoon period of our relationship. Today was no different. I was out in the corridor on the phone with Riya and Krish and Madhur were watching *House* in my room. I was whispering sweet nothings to Riya when Krish came out looking for me.

'Dude hang up and come inside quickly.' He said a little hassled.

'*Kya hua?*' I asked

'Something very very important man. Come ASAP.' He said and went inside.

Although I didn't wanna hang up on Riya I told her that something important had come up and I had to go and that I would call her up tomorrow. She said that it was okay and we hung up. I got inside my room and asked Krish what the dire emergency was.

'Madhur here is saying ki *Solid pak raha hai boss.* He is getting very bored.' Krish said.

'So?' I said getting a little angry. Surely this could wait.

'So he says that we don't do anything fun. And that we keep lazing like pigs every day.' Krish continued.

'Isn't DOTA and movies enough fun for you Madhur. What do you want us to do, dance for you?' Now I was really getting pissed.

'What's with your mood man? Had a fight with Riya or what?' Madhur asked

'No *re*. As a matter of fact I was on the verge of having phone sex when you assholes called me in...and that too for this.' I said putting the reason for my snobby behavior out in the open.

Madhur looked at Krish...Krish looked at Madhur...then both of them looked at me...then Madhur looked at Krish as Krish was looking at me and then vice versa. I smelled something really fishy as they were behaving in a very cocky way which is unlike them.

'What the fuck is the matter with the both of you' I asked.

They continued with their random staring thing for some more time.

'Whattttt' I asked managing a small laugh out of this irritating behavior. Finally Krish spilled it out.

'*uhhhh....Goa chalega?*' He asked.

'Are you serious' I asked a little concerned thinking that they had probably lost it.

'Ya obviously dude. Come on. We have a lot of free time now...nothing important is happening in college as well and we are in Bombay after all. *Bombay aake Goa nahi gaye to kya kiya*' Madhur popped in matter-of-factly.

'And this is the fun of it dude. A spontaneous plan works out best. *Bohot tafri aa rahi hai yaar.*' Krish added. It was a very luring proposition. I mean I was totally buying it. After all every one of us had seen *Dil Chahta Hai* and every guy has a dream of going to Goa with his friends after seeing that movie. Goa meant an amazing getaway to serene beaches with bikini clad women...cheap duty free alcohol...water sports...long bike rides on open roads with coconut and cashew trees all around. I had been to Goa a lot of times with my parents to know it in and out. But that was different...we always stayed at five star resorts amongst classy people...I never got to drink or ride a bike. I was in for sure.

'When do we leave' I asked

'In two days. Tomorrow we will call up our parents and talk to them and get the cash. I think fifteen grand for four days will be sufficient.' Krish said.

'Ya sure. I will talk to dad…he has a patient who owns some accommodation place in Candolim. He might be able to get us a good deal.' I said all jumpily.

So it was finalized…we were going to Goa…now all that remained was getting the permission of our parents and getting the budget approved.

I waited till late in the evening the next day before I called Dad. I had waited for Krish and Madhur to confirm the Goa trip from their side. After both of them gave a nod I called up dad. Convincing dad was a cake walk. He was thrilled that we were finally taking up some responsibility to make good use of our time. My mom on the other hand had her issues with the whole plan.

'Don't do anything that you might regret' she had said.

I promised her that all fun will be well within limits and she needn't worry. I told dad to transfer the fifteen grand in my account by tomorrow and talk to Reggie Uncle about the hotel bookings. He said that he will SMS me my booking details as soon as it is done and hung up.

The next day we decided that we would travel by bus to Goa. We went to Vashi where the booking office for the bus was to get the reservations done. Our mood was really upbeat and we were really looking forward to having a hell of a vacation. That night I broke the news of Goa to Riya. She voiced her own concerns.

'How the hell am I supposed to stay four days without talking to you baby' she said

I know it sounds very irritating...I mean every guy wants his space...and such kind of talk makes you feel pretty cramped for space. But when you are in those early days of a relationship everyone has his own insecurities. In such early times all you want to do is be close to your better half spending as much time with him as possible. I guess that is why I totally understood her and empathized with a 'I will call you every day *na* sweetheart. *Waise bhi* Bombay or Goa what difference does it make when I have to talk to you on the phone itself' speech.

'But you will be with your friends *na* baby. I don't want you to spoil your vacation by thinking about calling me all the time. You only call me if you get some free time okay.' I don't know from where she got this mature insight all of a sudden...but I guess when such things are said to you...your love for that person increases unconditionally.

'You are awesome, you know sweetheart. There can't be anyone as awesome as you. You are the epitome of awesomeness.' I said quite genuinely.

'I know that *re*. Tell me something new sweetie.' And with that we continued with our long-distance-over the phone-romance like every other day into the night.

That night I slept with dreams of paradise in my eyes. The paradise was Goa. I and Riya were lying down on the sandy beach. It was evening and the sun was fading away at the horizon. Right next to us were Krish and Aisha sitting with folded knees looking at each other laughing. At another corner was Madhur enjoying a walk by the beach with a *Firang* babe. Everyone seemed so happy. I was happy. I was with the people who really mattered to me. People who made living my life seem worthwhile. Everything seemed so real and blissed. I turned my head towards Riya and asked her whether this was a dream or was this what heaven felt like. She just smiled at me and said that this is as good as it gets. I told her that I loved her and we kissed. Life seemed so complete…if only in a dream.

12
FRIENDS FOREVER

January 2009

'*Bhaiya* eight Kingfisher mild *ke* small cans' Krish was telling the guy at the wine shop. We were at Heena Wines near Nerul Station. Tarun *bhai* who was our senior was coming with us to see us off at the bus station.

'All the time you are in Goa don't stay in your senses guys. Beer is cheaper than water there so make it a point to stay tipsy all the time' he had told us. It was his idea to have beer before we began our trip. So there we were three guys departing on this mad guy's trip to Goa drinking beer to celebrate our departure.

We reached the bus stop in Vashi at 11 PM. Our bus was getting loaded. We bade Tarun *bhai* a good bye and boarded the bus. We got seats in the second last row. I have always hated bus journeys. They remind me of that horrible summer when my parents had taken me to Daman and Diu with a whole lot of family friends. I had been motion sick throughout our bus journey and kept vomiting out of the windows in those last couple of rows. I have dreaded bus rides ever since. This was different though. It was a nice bus…one of those AC Volvos…although there wasn't much leg space and it felt kind of cramped…once the seats were reclined there wasn't much of a problem. The bus departed in a short while and finally we were on our way to Goa. The conductor came to check our tickets and give us blankets when the bus hit the Goa highway. Shortly after that the TV in the bus was turned on and they played Salman Khan's *Wanted*. It was one of those movies that we had missed owing to its stupid nature and a cheesy trailer. But now with nothing better to do on this twelve hour journey we decided to watch it anyway.

The bus entered Mapusa Goa at 11 AM. That was the stop we got off. The bus stop was in the core city of Mapusa and the whole feel of the city was surreal. It was very different from Bombay or Nagpur. We were at a circle with a lot of small shops selling cashews and a lot of local artifacts that surrounded a fountain which was at the center of the circle. We got our luggage and moved towards the taxi stand as our bus zoomed off toward Panjim. We hired a cab to take us to our hotel. I had never really stayed in this part of Goa before. Whenever I had come to Goa with my parents we would mostly stay either at Cida De Goa which was in Panjim or some other resort in south Goa which included the likes of…Majorda Beach Resort…The Taj Exotica…The Leela or The Holiday Inn. I guess the only five star resort that north Goa boasted of was The Taj Aguada Fort. The vast differences between North and South Goa were very evident. South Goa was all serene and had open fields of coconut and cashew trees which were free from any kind of habitation. It had wonderfully big churches and roads that ended in inland waters so to move on you had to take the ferries. North Goa on the other hand was densely populated and on either side of the roads which were narrower and had more traffic you could see a lot of restaurants serving sea food. As we drove towards our hotel we saw a lot of *goras* walking shirtless going all pink under the Goa sun. I guess this was the place you visited with your friends and leave south Goa for the times with your family.

The cab dropped us outside our hotel. There was a huge stone entrance to the hotel which had Reggie's Holiday Homes painted on it in navy blue. We went inside to see a decent sized swimming pool which had a lot of beach chairs around it on which some *goras* were sunbathing. There was the hotel's restaurant right next to the pool. The bar at the restaurant had a huge refrigerator with a transparent glass door. Through it you could see all the Kingfisher Mild Beer bottles kept inside. The temperature wasn't that high… it was a very sunny day and was very humid. All of us agreed that it wouldn't be a bad idea to grab a chilled beer right away. But first we had to check in…so we went up to the reception.

'Hi Sir. May I help you?' A tall dark lean guy wearing a Hawaiian style shirt standing behind the reception guy asked us.

'Yes…we have a reservation here under name of Aman Sarin from Bombay.' I told him.

'Yes sir…we have been expecting you. Please follow me. Reggie sir would like to meet with you.' He said as he led us into a cabin that had a nice wooden door which shone from a lot of polishing. We stood outside as the guy from the reception peaked inside and said 'Sir...Mr Aman Sarin is here.'

'Oh please send them in' said the voice from behind the door and the guy held the door open for us.

As we entered I saw the familiar looking Reggie Uncle get up from his seat and come toward me with open arms. He was a man in his late forties had a receding hairline, a nose fat as a potato, and a pot belly. He was dressed in an oversized T shirt and track pants which totally put him in the holidaying groove. I had seen a lot of Reggie uncle when I was growing up. He used to own a restaurant in Nagpur where I and my family ate out loads of times. He was my dad's patient at first but then became a close family friend and was a frequent visitor at our place for get-togethers. He had sold off his restaurant some five years ago and had come to Goa and opened up this hotel. '*Kaise ho betaji*' he said as he hugged me tightly.

'I am fine uncle. How are you? You look so young and dashing *uncleji*. Goa is really suiting you.' I said amicably

'What *yaar betaji*...I am going to cross half century next year. Now I am no more the happy go lucky Reggie uncle you used to know.' He said very matter-of-factly.

'So how is business uncle? Last month must have been killer right...with Christmas and New Year's.' I asked.

'It was very exhausting *betaji*. We were all booked throughout the month. Now that it's finally over I have some breathing space.' He said.

I introduced him to Krish and Madhur and they exchanged pleasantries.

'And where are your girlfriends shirlfriends huh? I thought you will come with all girls whirls.' Reggie uncle asked naughtily.

'What girlfriends Reggie uncle? We also need some time away from them *na*. This is a guys only thing.' I said. '*Accha* listen Reggie uncle one more thing I want to ask you.'

'Ya say *na beta.*' He said intently

'You are not going to report anything that happens here back home *na?*' this was something that had struck me as a disadvantage at staying at a family friend's hotel.

'Of course not *betaji*. It will all be between us. It's all a part of the…what you say…resident-hotel owner-relationship. And after all we were also young like you and went out with our friends when we were in college. We *toh* didn't even tell our parents. I totally understand. After all what happens in Goa stays in Goa *rightji.*' His words were very comforting and laid my fears to rest.

'Absolutely' the three of us chirped happily.

He then took us to the place where we would be staying. It was one of the many two storied bungalows that looked identical and were built in two parallel rows. On the ground floor was a kitchen which had a fridge, a microwave and a stove. On the first floor was one bedroom, a hall and a bathroom. On the second floor was another bedroom with an attached bathroom and an open terrace. From the terrace you could see the pool on one side…the terraces of the other houses in front where we saw a foreigner couple sitting and reading their newspaper. The woman looked at me, smiled 'Hey how are you' she said.

'Fantastic' I replied and smiled back. On the other side I could see the Candolim public beach which had a lot of shacks and beach chairs on it.

'It is the best public beach in North Goa *betaji*' Reggie uncle said standing next to me. 'You like the place?' he asked.

The place was amazing. Right now I was finding it way better than all the five star resorts I had ever stayed in. 'Five star' I told him. It was the perfect bachelor pad I thought. If only I could stay here forever. I told Reggie uncle that we would need three bikes to roam around in Goa. He asked us for our driving licenses and told us that he would take care of it.

After he left we got unpacked. I and Krish decided to share the room on the second floor and left the first floor room for Madhur. It was a decision that was made out of considerate behavior towards Madhur. I and Krish were committed in a relationship...so if Madhur who was the only free bird in the girls department somehow got lucky...he could have his privacy. He had fought for the second floor room very hard but I and Krish made it very clear that if we could not google then at least we could ogle...if you know what I mean. After we finished unpacking it was finally time to get that chilled beer we so desperately wanted. We called room service and ordered for three pints of Kings Beer which is the local beer of Goa. It came pretty quickly and we made a huge toast to Goa and the next three days of crazy ass fun.

Reggie uncle had managed to get us two Avengers and one Dio to ride around Goa. We thanked him and drove off to Anjuna beach. Anjuna beach was a nice quiet beach way up north. The ride from

Candolim to Anjuna was nice. The roads weren't very crowded and the three of us comfortably cruised here taking our own sweet time as we breathed in the sweet Goa air and everything that came with it. The beach was rocky and a steep slope led to it. We decided that we wouldn't hit the beach and instead sit at Anjuna Xpress which was a restaurant which had a bamboo shack like feel to it since it was lunch time already and we were starving. We placed our order of fried prawns, fish fry and three Kingfishers with the waiter and sat down on the outer parapet of the restaurant from where you could see the beach beneath you. The sea breeze was gently blowing. And as we felt the breeze in our hair and on our face it brought up a feeling of eternal bliss. The songs played at the restaurant were all SRK's top chartbusters…from *Do dil mil rahe hai* to *Jaadoo teri nazar*…from *Kal ho na ho* to *Na jaane mere dil ko kya ho gaya* all those songs that were so engraved on those sweet memories of growing up were played and it felt magical. Three best friends, Goa, amazing weather, lip smacking food, beer and SRK songs…the perfect vacation…in short…heaven.

After we finished our lunch we checked out the shops. All of us had to buy some beach wear. It was so totally ironical as three guys who wound never go shopping at Bandra Linkin Road or Fashion Street were out buying clothes at a place that was even cheaper. We got ourselves a pair of capris and some T-shirts saying 'GO GOA' and we were happy. Next we went up to a street side vendor who was selling sunglasses for 99 rupees a pair. We all bought a pair each. Madhur and Krish got what were some good Aviator copies and I got myself a copy of what Vivek Oberoi had sported in *Kyuu…Ho gaya na.*

Next up we went to a Body Art shop. Apparently that shop was pretty famous as it had pictures of the owner with top end Bollywood celebrities pinned up on its walls. From Sushmita Sen to Bipasha Basu everyone graced the wall with their presence. We thought getting a temporary tattoo wouldn't be a very bad idea and thus scanned through the brochure for the design we wanted. The artist was very creative and helped us pick our design according to our body type. I got an angry bull's face with flaring nostrils and crooked eyebrows done on my right arm. It resembled the Brahma Bull of The Rock by all angles. Dwayne Johnson a.k.a. The Rock had always been my favorite wrestler...so getting the bull which was the same tattoo he had on his arm painted on my arm too made me feel like yelling... 'IF YOU SMELLLL (tongue wagging madly) ...What The Rock (a long pause)...Is Cooking. Krish got a lycan's (a wolf's) face done on his right arm and Madhur got some chinese letters done on his. All the three of us were really happy with our tattoos and even lined up displaying our tattoos to get our pictures clicked.

The sun was setting in the far horizon into the sea and we decided to drive to Panjim. The bus ride had been very tiring and we had decided to get a train back to Bombay three days from now. The train booking office was in Panjim and so were all the good liquor stores, so we decided to buy all the liquor that we had to carry back today itself. The ride to Panjim was good. The roads were broad and once we reached the highway, riding our bikes felt great. After crossing the bridge we entered Panjim after sunset. The streets looked familiar as I had spent a lot of time in Panjim when I had come here last with my parents. I called Prateek who was a friend of mine from school and was studying Engineering in BITS Goa. He told me the names of all the good wine shops in Panjim and also briefed me on some good restaurants nearby. After getting our tickets booked on The Konkan Kanya we went up to Tony's Wine Shoppe. We brought a bottle of Smirnoff Green Apple Vodka…a bottle of Devar's White Label Whiskey…a bottle of Haig. The list ended with the bomb item…something that we had seen in the movie Eurotrip and had wanted try ever since…a drink that was banned in many major countries for its hallucinogenic high…it was the green fairy…a bottle of Absinthe.

After the liquor shopping was over we parked our bikes and set out walking around Panjim to find out the restaurant Prateek had told me we shouldn't miss.

'Dude there is no place in Goa where you will get food like Goodinio's' he had said. So after walking around for some twenty odd minutes and asking our way around we finally reached the place.. We walked inside into a dimly lit room. It resembled something that I thought pubs used to look like in the early nineteenth century. There was a huge eating area with not many tables. The tables were big and round with just four chairs on each table. There was a huge space between two tables. The ambiance was nice…the place was illuminated by only a half a dozen zero watt bulbs…no tube lights or fancy modern day CFLs. There was an antic jukebox at the corner which was playing old R&B songs mostly Air Supply and all. Wow…I thought to myself…they still make places like these…it's great.

'This place is totally kickass' Krish said as if he had read my mind. We took a table in the center of the hall and sat down. The waiter got us the menu and we received another shock. Everything was so fucking cheap it was almost hard to believe. A plate of tiger prawns cost only 60 bucks. We practically ordered everything on the menu thinking that perhaps the quantity would be less…but then another shock. It was huge…a dish each and we were stuffed. I remember that we even had to ask them to cancel half of the order. The food was yumm and I couldn't help myself from calling up Prateek the moment we left to thank him for telling us about this awesome place.

We got back to our hotel at 10.30 PM and Reggie uncle who was sitting by the poolside drinking some beer greeted us. He asked us how our day was and we showed him our tattoos and told him about Goodinio's. We also showed him all the liquor shopping we had done. He got a little scared after looking at the Absinthe bottle and told us not to over drink it as it was some very strong stuff. He told us the right way to consume Absinthe which was not by making pegs with Sprite. We thanked him for the knowledge and got back to our room. We pulled out chairs and sat on the terrace. I looked over at the terrace of the house opposite ours. Some trance music was being played. The curtains were drawn and behind them we could see the shadows of two people making love. We decided to have some Absinthe and retire into the night as we were pretty tired. We opened the bottle got three spoons and some sugar cubes. The sugar cubes were kept on the spoons and then the Absinthe was poured over it. The sugar gently melted and dissolved in the green liquid and our drink was ready. We raised our spoons and said 'cheers' and then gulped it down. It had the flavor of *sauf*…you know the sweet candy coated *sauf* they give you in the restaurants after your meal…it tasted just like that. But as it passed down my esophagus and into my stomach…I felt as if my entire GI tract was on fire. It was just like the feeling when you gulp down Vodka or Tequila neat but only more intense. After about ten minutes we decided to do another round and prepared the drink on the spoons. This time it went down more smoothly. All the three of us kept sitting there on the terrace listening to "Principles of Lust" being played from the house opposite ours and kept staring at the moon. I don't know how long we sat there but no one spoke a word. Slowly the moon turned from a bright yellow to light green. The dark black night was still dark but no longer black…it was dark green. I looked around and felt as if someone had used photo shop on my world and had turned the Sepia Green effect on.

'Is it just me or are you guys also seeing everything green.' I asked still blinking and hoping everything would be alright.

'Esss man tohtalli…everythin is so gleeenn.' Madhur said in an abnormally slurred speech. I and Krish looked at Madhur and started laughing out loud. 'Bhy al you guysss lawfing?' he asked. And that made us laugh more. And then as if he was missing out on the fun even Madhur started laughing. We laughed like mad men for minutes together and somehow laughing was unstoppable. As soon as we managed to get silent for a few seconds we would exchange glances and start laughing again. Now besides living in a green world I was even feeling high. My head was totally spinning and I made it a point to spin with it. We danced and danced and for a while when I was dancing I thought Krish and Madhur were even making out. But I was too busy doing my own stuff to bother. That night the last thing

I remember is receiving two phone calls. The first one I know was from Tarun *bhai* who asked if we were in our senses or sloshed. I had told him that we were completely out. The second one was from Riya which I know now because I had checked the call log next morning. I personally have no clue what I spoke to her about but from what she told me the conversation had went something like this.

'Hi baby what's up…having fun' she had asked.

'Are you The Green Fairy…I love you Green Fairy' I had muttered absently.

Over the next two days we enjoyed Goa and everything it had to provide. We indulged in jet skiing, surfing, parasailing and all kinds of water sports. We lazed around on Candolim beach drinking beer on the beach chairs under the umbrellas. We ogled at the bikini clad *gori mems*. Ate so much sea food it could last us a life time. Then we spent one evening at the Aguada Fort looking at the sun making sweet love to the sea just like those three guys from *Dil Chahta Hai*. Rode on our bikes to south Goa and lit a candle at the churches. We went for the evening boat cruise from Panjim Harbour to Miramar beach enjoying the Goan music. It was a treat…all my favorite songs were played…from "Nothings Gonna Change my Love for You" to "Hello"…it was amazing. We fine dined one night at The Little Italy which had a great candle light setting and served the finest Port Wine. On the last night we went pubbing at Tito's. It was mad…I remember getting sloshed with more than ten pints of beer down my system…I had chatted up with a lot of cute looking chicks…and finally I had vomited blood into the sink in the men's washroom and had passed out next to it. This time I had spent in Goa with my friends has crossed my expectations by a huge margin...it had been total Mad-ass-OMFG Fun.

It was finally time for us to go back. Our train left at 4.30 PM from Margoa station. We had reached the station at 4 PM itself and were waiting on the platform for our train to arrive.

'Dude these three days were epic guys. It was just Legen...wait for it...dary' Krish said doing a Barney Stinson from *How I Met your Mother*.

'They totally were man.' I said

'And you know what the best part was' He asked

'I know...it was the night we got high on Absinthe and couldn't stop laughing and Madhur's slurred speech. Tohtalli Gleen' I said mocking Madhur over that night as I nudged his shoulder. He smiled goofily

'Ya that was fucking hilarious but that is not what I am talking about' Krish said intently

'Then what is it' Madhur asked.

'The best part was that I realized how lucky I am to have you guys as my friends.' I wanted to say something but he cut me short and continued. 'Never in my life have I felt as humbled as I have felt in the last couple of days. Even with Aisha I have never been so happy and care free as I was when I was here with you guys. You guys mean the world to me. And you Aman...I know we have had our difference in the past and that always made me look at you with an apprehensive view but today I am proud of myself that I have a friend like you in my life. I love you man' I could see the tears that had crept up into Krish's eyes as he said the last words and hugged me.

'I love you too man' I said feeling a little sentimental myself.

'You know the three of us should make another pact' Madhur said. 'At the end of our MBBS course we will come back to Goa to relive these days…just the three of us'

'Ya dude we definitely will. And why only after the course we will come here whenever we feel like getting away from our hectic life or when we miss each other after college is over. After all we are all friends for life.' Krish said and we all hugged each other.

The train coo cooed in and we boarded it for the seven hour long journey back to Bombay. What a trip this had been. They say that your college days are the best days of your life…That these days never come back. They say that the friends you make here last you a life time. I was having a blast…I had an amazing life…amazing friends…there was not much left to ask of life…it was like I was living a DREAM. But I guess that's the peculiar thing about DREAMS…they leave you with the bitter reality once you wake up.

13
IT'S ALL ABOUT THOSE THREE WORDS

Summer 2009

My first year university exams had ended a few weeks back. I was back home...back to Nagpur. The results had come in a and I had passed first year MBBS with flying colors. I had managed to get a decent 129 and 131 out of 200 in Physiology and Biochemistry respectively. But what I was really proud of was my 161 score in Anatomy which meant I had a distinction in the subject. The exams had been nothing but an utter slogfest. There had been long study hours and lots of sleepless night that were put in to make them seem like a cakewalk now. All I really wanted now was to lay low for a while and enjoy home. Over the months I had missed home like anything. The slow paced life in Nagpur...Mom's home made chicken...my dog...Riya. I was glad to be back in Nagpur.

All these days I spent a lot of time with my family. We used to sit together every night for dinner like one happy family and enjoy our nice conversations. I think it is all a part of growing up. As you grow up you tend to enjoy conversations with your parents…even those work related talks seem to be interesting which you used to hate when you were a teenager. And plus I was becoming a doctor like my parents so I could relate more to them. I discussed a lot of medical things with my Mom and Dad and they seemed very impressed on how I was picking up on things so quickly. They were very proud of me when my result had come out. I could see it in their eyes. My dad is a man of very few words. The only conversations that we do have when I'm in Bombay are about my expenses, money matters and some study related stuff. But that day when he had hugged me and said that he was proud of me I felt like he finally found the son he always wanted in me. I had never seen him so happy. Not even when I had won the National gold medal for swimming. And plus the fact that I was a very average student in class didn't help as he expected me to be among the top rankers. He never said anything about it but I always knew that, that was what he expected out of me. He also threw a huge party to celebrate my passing at The Pride Hotel. All our relatives and close family friends were present. And he had very proudly re-introduced me to everyone as 'Aman Sarin – The Doctor in the making – My Son'.

My mom on the other hand never has a shortage of words to express herself. And she went on about how I could have done better and got a distinction in all the subjects. I knew she was happy. Our family time used to extend late into the night and then as my parents went off to their dreamland I too would retreat into my room. Ever since I was a child my room has been my 'Devil's Workshop'. It had everything I needed to survive; from a TV to a fridge, all my necessities were met. It is the one place in this world where I can sit for hours together and think. Think about life and love and words and songs…think about me. Every night I would turn on the world space radio in my room and sit in my rocking chair as I got lost in thought about anything and everything.

The buzzing of my phone always brought me to reality every day. Sometimes it was Krish or Madhur or Aisha…but mostly it was Riya. I was meeting up with Riya after a long break of five months. I had dedicated all my evening time to Riya. We would go out on long drives…or go get coffee…or just enjoy a long walk along the roads of Civil Lines. But there was obviously a lot of catching up to do. I didn't mind talking to Riya over phone for hours together…in fact I rather liked it. But I guess what happens in a relationship when you have crossed a particular point…is that you always run out of topics to talk about. It's not that you have stopped loving the other person or have stopped caring for him…it's just that thing in your head which tells you 'what more can there possibly be to talk about.' And then starts those long series of phone calls where after a few minutes of talking there are long pauses whice are broken by 'So what else?' by one person…and most of the times the other person replies 'Nothing much you tell me.' And the conversation continues as neither one of you really wants to keep the phone down. It is very hard to believe that even when two people who are in love are not really talking somehow they just get immense happiness by just holding on for hours together on the phone. I guess it's mostly the whole psychological thing of having someone who cares for you with you that makes you feel all warm and cozy which in turn leads to happiness. I think the whole fact that one person feels safe and comforted by the other person is a reason enough for a lot of people to spend their entire lives together. Well if that was the case then my relationship with Riya had certainly reached that level. When I was in Bombay, Riya and I had discussed the possibility of sleeping together a lot of times. We had also indulged in quite a few phone sex conversations which had left us both wanting for more. But as of now I had been in Nagpur for over three weeks and nothing of that sort had really materialized.

It was around 2 PM in the afternoon and I was all alone at home. I was finishing my lunch as I sat in my room watching television when Riya called.

'Hi…what's up' I said as I picked up her call.

'Nothing you tell me.' She replied in a very standard not-much-to-talk-about kinda way.

'Was just finishing up with lunch sweetheart.' I told her

'Oh…so you are alone at home?' She inquired

'Ya…Mom and Dad are at work *na.*'

'Hmmmm' came the reply.

'What is that Hmmm supposed to mean?' I asked

'Do you mind if I come over? I'm getting really bored at home and I really want to meet you.' She said.

'Ya sure sweetie…come over…no issues.' I told her.

'Cool then I'll see you in half an hour' she said and we hung up.

I finished my lunch and cleaned up my room as it was in a mess and had a quick bath. She rang the doorbell at around 2.45 PM. She gave me a peck on my cheek as I opened the door to let her in. We went up to my room. She sat on the bed and I took my seat on my rocking chair.

'So what's up' I asked her…well that is the way I opened every conversation with her.

'Nothing I was just missing you a lot and couldn't wait till the evening so I thought I would come over. It is good that you are alone at home.' She said

'Hmmmm…So what do you wanna do?' I asked her

'I don't know ya…nothing in particular. I just wanna spend some time with you.' She replied.

'Okay'

And then followed a long silence. It was pretty long…I guess long enough to make us both uncomfortable. So I got up and went up to my desk 'Music?' I asked.

'Ya sure' she said. I turned on my World Space Radio and tuned in to the forty on forty channel. I sat down on the desk itself as it was right next to my bed and thus was closer to her. The sound of 'It Ends Tonight' by All American Rejects was the only thing that could be heard for the next couple of minutes.

Then as the song changed to 'What Goes Around Comes Around' by Justin Timberlake she patted her right hand on the bed signaling me to come and sit next to her. I complied with her gesture and sat down on the bed next to her. She slowly put her hand and on my hand and held it firmly. I looked at her and met her eyes which were looking at me. We looked into each-other's eyes and in that moment her eyes said the same thing that my eyes were trying to say. I leaned in towards her with a slightly tilted head and she responded by covering the distance between us and our lips met. She tasted like strawberry or maybe that was just her lip gloss but whatever it was it felt amazing. We landed soft kisses on each-other's lips. I could feel her breath on my neck and it felt amazing. I think the feeling was mutual as the gentle kissing soon turned passionate and tongues started tangling. Soft kisses were now hard wet kisses and our hands started wandering. Her hand was playing with my hair and my hand caressing her cheek. She moved and put her hand around my neck and pulled me close rather strongly. Her tongue was twirling in my mouth and reaching places not even I knew existed…I sucked on her tongue as it felt great. Her left hand was around my neck and was choking me a little. The little asphyxia was turning me on more and more. I was running out of breath and from the way she was breathing I knew so was she…but we were so into each-other that neither one of us wanted to let go. Her right hand had moved under my shirt and with her palm she was caressing my chest and my left nipple. I too let my hand slip beneath her top and started caressing her back. I think it turned her on as she broke the kiss and let her head fall back while still holding me close. She was panting…her mouth open and letting out soft moans. I started kissing her neck gently and her rate of breathing increased. Her hand was still choking me…turning me on every minute. With her other hand she was pinching my nipple slightly which wasn't helping either. My hand found the buckle of her bra and I unhooked it. She fell down on the bed on her back and drew me with her. I went over her and kept kissing her neck more intensely now and gave it a little bite every now and then. She let out a little moan with every bite which was so sexy I couldn't stop myself.

Then after a few minutes she said 'Go lower.' I obliged as I went down kissing her cleavage ignoring her breasts all together. I lingered over her abdomen for a while as I kissed her around her belly button. Then I took the liberty of unbuttoning and unzipping her jeans as I slid them off her. I was kissing her right thigh now...softly and gently...slow, wet, gentle kisses down her thigh and on her right knee. I lifted her leg and planted kisses on her calf muscles and then all the way down to her toes. She was a beautiful Goddess and I wanted to savor her. Oh! she was so sexy. And I could tell she was enjoying this attention. I went on my way up again. I guess she thought that the clothes were no longer necessary as she pulled me up and pulled off my T-shirt over my head and removed her top and bra too. She had nice petite breasts with rose pink nipples. I gently kissed her breasts one at a time avoiding the nipples. 'Gosh Aman you are such a tease' she said. As I kissed her nipple and twirled my tongue over her areola she let out a loud moan and dug her nails into my back which made me finch with pain. But it was a sweet and sensuous pain that did nothing but turn me on even more. I kissed my way down and rested on her inner thighs. She spread her legs a little urging me to go for her love hole but I was more than happy being the tease for now. I could see that the crotch of her panties had got wet with her juices and could smell her sweet aroma. As tempting as it looked I kept teasing her by kissing and licking her inner thigh. 'Oh baby...you make me feel so sexy' she moaned out. She finally pushed me off and lost her panties and lay back for me to continue. I looked deep into her eyes and then moved closer to her and kissed her as I slid one finger into her vagina. She moaned into my mouth and shivered a little. Then I slowly entered her with my finger as my thumb massaged her clitoris. Her moans became louder and breathing grew intense. I moved down between her legs and placed my face in front of her love hole. I think I was breathing over her as she shivered a little. I gently lapped up her vagina and flicked my tongue over her clitoris and sucked it. 'Oh ya suck it harder baby' she said 'bite it' as she put both her hand on my head and pulled my face inside her. I was feeling smothered but I didn't give up. And then within minutes her body shuddered into an intense orgasm. I almost felt as if she was having a convulsion as she shivered lying down on my bed. I held her tightly and asked if she was alright. She didn't say anything just laid there with her eyes closed hugging me closely. Finally after a few minutes she looked up at me and smiled.

'That is the best foreplay can get.' She said. 'I didn't know my boyfriend was such an expert in the art of love making.'

'Well there are two reasons for it' I said proudly. 'Firstly I have read a lot of Sidney Sheldon's books so you pick up the technical detail from there. Secondly for the practical point of view I sleep with a lot of women.' With that I gave her a wicked smile and she elbowed me hard in the ribs. 'Awww…that hurt.'

'Well now that you have taken such good care of me…let me look at you.' She said and moved her hand toward my crotch and slid down track pants. 'Oh…we have quite a man down here' she said as she wrapped her hand around the bulge in my boxers.

We made wild passionate love till it was getting dark outside. And then as we lay down next to each other all spent…she whispered into my ear 'Aman I love you.' My eyes were fixed on the rotating fan on the ceiling. I was amidst a hurricane of emotions. Next to me was this beautiful girl that I really loved and I swear to god I did. We had shared something really intimate together and it was beautiful. I told her that I loved her too…a lot. But then she came over me and looked right into my eyes.

'Don't you ever leave me. I am too much in love with you to imagine life without you. Don't you ever hurt me because if you do I swear to god…I will fucking kill you.' I guess it was just the beauty of the moment and her hormones which were talking. I nodded back.

All every guy really wants to hear at the end of the day are those three magical words after all… which make everything else seem worthwhile. And no they certainly are not I LOVE YOU. The three magical words are…LET'S GET NAKED…it's all about the hickeys and hormones after all.

14

WISH YOU A HAPPY LONELY NEW YEAR

December 2009

People say you should never be alone on New Year's Eve. I hardly can understand why New Year's has to be such a big deal. Why is it that you need a girl with you on this day? Is it because at the stroke of midnight you just hold her and kiss her the way they show you in those romantic comedy Hollywood movies. Why can't a guy not have a date for New Year's? And why is it that if he does not have one then people look at him as if he were some loser.

For me this New Year's was just about that. I was all by myself at this night club in Bombay. All my friends had gone back home and since I had to do a better job than just sitting alone in my hostel room and getting drunk all by myself, I had decided to come out.

I don't know why people say night life in Bombay is amazing. I mean what is so great about coming to such places which are so jam packed with people that you hardly have space to breathe. How do people enjoy dancing within such close proximity with sweaty bodies? What really is the fun of being in a room which has deafening music being played so you can't hear your own voice? If this is what fun meant to people then I certainly wasn't one of them.

I decided to go get myself a beer to loosen out a bit. The bar was so crowded that it took me around ten minutes to get the bartender's attention. Finally having got my beer I headed towards the sofa at the corner of the club. Suddenly I realized that this is why you should never be alone on New Year's. The whole world is out there celebrating in front of you with their loved ones and here you are all by yourself getting bored alone drinking beer. I finished my drink and got myself on the dance floor as the music was suddenly sounding better. The DJ was playing "we are in heaven by DJ Sammy". It is one of those songs that gets me grooving. After fifteen minutes of dancing I felt I was being stared at. As I looked around I saw hundreds of people looking at me and giggling to themselves. I thought that there were only two reasons why that would be happening. Either I was dancing stupidly and or I was dancing alone and looking like a complete loser. I knew I danced well and that made me believe that it had to be reason two. Feeling like a complete idiot and knowing that coming here alone was a big mistake I moved away from the dance floor. According to a certain friend of mine only three types of people would dance alone. A) Hyperactive young kids B) absolutely drunk adults and C) desperate young guys trying to get close to drunk girls. I knew I didn't fit into any of these three categories so I decided that the only way I could get my four thousand rupees entry fee worth was by getting drunk.

After waiting another ten minutes at the bar I took two beers and headed for that sofa again. This time there were people sitting there. There was this man in his mid-40's I presumed sitting with a pretty girl that would be his daughter's age. But here in this dimly lit room with disco lights flashing, no one seemed to bother. I finished my drinks standing by the exit door with the bouncer who seemed like the only other person there who was alone like me. But in no time I saw his companion- another bouncer come along. Was there no one like me who was in here alone.

I decided I needed a smoke so I got myself to this balcony where smoking wasn't prohibited. I lit up my Classic Mild's and leaned over the railing looking at Bombay lost in celebration when I felt someone tap my shoulder.

'Excuse me, can I get a light?'

She was this mind blowing gorgeous girl wearing a blue strapless dress up to her knees. She had a Davidoff lights between her lips.

'Ya sure. Here you go.' I said helping her with my lighter

'Thanks.' She stood next to me leaning over that railing.

After about thirty seconds she finally spoke 'you dance very well.'

'Oh come on you can't be serious.'

'No seriously I was looking at you for like those ten minutes you were on the dance floor. And I think you did a great job.'

'Thanks for the compliments but I think I am done for the night with dancing.'

'And why is that?'

I told her about my friend's theory of the three types of people who dance alone in public. She simply laughed.

'Dude that's crazy. You should do what you want to, not what everyone else expects of you. How many people do you know out there who you are going to meet tomorrow? And plus you are way better than most of the people in there.'

'Thanks, I am Aman by the way.'

'Ok hi Aman by the way.'

'And you are?'

'I will tell you my name if you will get back in there and dance.'

'Hey come on why are you so keen on making me dance.'

'*Aaivehi*'

'*Aaivehi..?*'

'Yup.'

'*Theek hai*. I will dance if you dance with me.'

'Hey I can't dance.'

'Of course you can. Everybody can dance. Let's go in there and show the people how it is done.'

'Fine, after all I can't deprive the dance floor of a good dancer like you. And ya I am Preeti.'

'It's a pleasure meeting you Preeti.'

'Trust me the pleasure is all mine. Now let's dance. I am dying to make a fool of you after you see I can't dance'

'We'll see about that. Let's go.'

Preeti was right, she couldn't dance. All she was doing was snapping her fingers and moving her head. But no matter what she was doing she looked fabulous. After dancing to three tracks she moved in closer to me and put her head against my cheek and yelled in my ear.

'I told you I can't dance.'

I smiled back at her. Then five seconds later yelled back.

'That's ok, you are doing great.' She smiled back.

'I think I need a drink.' She said about ten seconds later.

'Ya I need one too.'

So we got off the dance floor and she told me she would like a Long Island Ice Tea. I told her I would get her one. It was 11.30 and practically everyone was on the dance floor by this time so the bar was empty. I got the Long Island Ice Tea for her and a beer for myself. With the drinks we went out to the balcony to get away from the noise.

'You see the city out there Aman. Isn't it just amazing how it looks from here?'

'Yes, I just love the way Bombay looks at night, especially Marine Drive.'

'I don't know why I love this city so much Aman. Even after knowing that there is a whole big ruthless conniving world out there. Are you from Bombay Aman?

'No I am from Nagpur.'

'Well that's good then. At least you wouldn't be like those bastards who breaks a girl's heart on New Year's.'

'You know what! I don't have a clue of what you're talking about.'

And then she told me about Mihir. Mihir was her boyfriend. He was the one with whom she had come to this party. She told me how crazily she was in love with him. And how a stupid fight was responsible for their breakup just a few hours ago right on this balcony.

'Who does that Aman? Who breaks up with his girlfriend on New Year's Eve?'

Now I am not that great at handling emotional girls. Especially when those emotions aren't for me. I mean I can be all fake and tell them all goody goody stuff and make them feel better. But not this time. All I could say was 'I don't.'

She didn't respond much to that and I was glad she didn't. After an eternity of silence she finally spoke again

'So do you have a girlfriend Aman?'

Now I was kind of expecting this conversation to go this way.

'Yes, as a matter of fact I do.'

'Oh! I see.'

Her reply kind of took me by surprise. What did she mean? Did I look like a guy who can't have a girlfriend?

'uhh…What is that supposed to mean?'

'Oh! It's nothing. I thought you wouldn't.'

'And why is that?'

'It's just that you are celebrating New Year's by yourself made me think that you probably were single. So is she from your college?'

'No. Not from my college. She is in Nagpur. You know long distance relationship.'

'Oh! Long distance relationship huh? Do people still do that these days?'

'Don't know much about people but I certainly am in one.'

'Does it really work out for you people?'

'I don't know. Let's just say we are working on it.'

'Good for you.'

It was 11.58 PM. Just two more minutes before I would be ringing in the New Year with a girl I had just met two hours ago.

'Hey do you think we can catch up with each other someday later. Maybe I could call you.' She said

'Ya totally.'

We exchanged phone numbers and promised to be in touch. Then just as I was going to bend forward and kiss her on the cheek and wish her a Happy New Year's.

'Hey Babe.'

It was a guy standing right behind me in a black suit.

'Hi Mihir. What are you doing here?'

'Babe I am sorry. I really love you. And I realized how stupid I was leaving you today. I went over to Kenny's and I saw our pictures of school and I remembered what you mean to me. We are meant for each other. We have always been together through thick and thin. If only you would forgive me I promise I will make it up to you. I love you Preeti.'

'I love you too Mihir.'

They hugged each other. The lights were switched off. The countdown began.

Everyone yelled in unison '10...9...8...7 '

I didn't want to be the guy that was going to be left alone this New Year in a place where everyone had someone for themselves. I left Preeti and Mihir on that balcony. I left those hundred people in that Disc and I walked out of the door and onto the streets. I could hear people wishing their loved ones a Happy New Year. The sky lit up with fireworks. It was an amazing sight. I stood there on the middle of the street and took out a cigarette lit it up and looked up at the brightly colored sky and said to myself.

'Happy New Year Aman. Happy New Year.'

After I drove back to my hostel and parked my car in the lot I stood in front of my college. The magnificent thirteen storied building stood in front of me with the board saying Dr.D.Y.Patil Medical College. It had been more than a year since I moved to Mumbai and took admission in this college. And this time had been nothing short of phenomenal. I must say I still remembered my first day of college and my first day in the hostel. My first medical lecture, my first college crush, and my first ragging session, all these memories were still so fresh in my head. I had come a long way since then but those memories started reeling in front of me. I was drunk and I felt tipsy. I felt my head go heavy. My vision started blurring out. My stomach felt funny and in no time I threw up. Somehow I thought this probably wasn't the alcohol. There was something about all this that made me feel there was something inside me that was going wrong. Soon my thinking was laid to rest. My legs couldn't hold me anymore. My eyes couldn't stay open anymore. I just couldn't think anymore. The only thing I do remember from that time onwards is that I fainted and collapsed.

15
BABE...WE SLEPT TOGETHER

January 2010

My phone was ringing. I paused the episode of 'How I Met Your Mother' that I was watching on my laptop to see who was calling. It was Riya. I picked it up.

'Hey babe! What's up?'

'Hi, what are you doing?' she sounded a bit off.

'Nothing just finished dinner and got back to the hostel.' I lied.

'Okay...so when were you planning to call me?'

'Well I just got out of the washroom. I overate *toh bohot pressure aa raha tha*. I was just going to call you.' I lied again.

'Oh come on Aman don't lie to me.' Now she sounded more angry than irritated.

'Why would I lie to you sweetheart.' I said trying to play it cool.

'Aman I just read your status update on Facebook saying how cool

119

you find 'How I Met Your Mother' and Neil Patrick Harris. It was posted fifteen minutes back. You were watching that stupid show na?' she was really mad now.

'Don't you dare shout at me Riya. Yes I was watching the show. And I can't help it if you find it stupid. I like it. At least it is better than fighting with you every night.' I realized being on the defensive wasn't the best option here.

'So you want to say that I am the one who picks fights with you every night.'

'Well it sure seems that way. I think you really enjoy picking fights with me. You tend to make a big deal out of everything.'

'Well I'm sorry if you feel that way but you are the one who has no time for me these days. At night either you are having dinner or driving or watching a movie. And during the day you are mostly playing that stupid game DOTA or just busy with your friends. Where do I fit in your life Aman? I really need to know what has been wrong with you lately. Because from what I see it looks like you are just running away from your responsibilities towards me now that the honeymoon period of our relationship is over.' Her voice was now cracking up and it looked like she might start crying any moment now.

'I can't help it if you feel that way Riya. I always told you that this is going to be tough. With you in Nagpur and me here in Mumbai it was always going to be tough. I can't really fit you into each and every second of my day you know. And with this attitude of yours it's not getting any better.' I thought I was coming down too heavy on her but I was determined not to fall for her crying.

'I am not asking you to fit me in each and every second of your life goddamit. But at least give me something to live with. I know I can't see you every day and I am fine with it. The least you can do Aman is to just talk to me for a few minutes. When was the last time that we had a meaningful conversation? When was the last time we had a conversation? For the past one month all we have been doing is fighting. You didn't even pick up my call on our anniversary. You didn't even call me on our anniversary. Fucking you forgot the day when we pledged unconditional love for each other. I know you couldn't have been that drunk that you slept the whole day. I want to know what's wrong with you Aman. What is it that has made you so cold and inconsiderate? I need answers Aman.' She was crying now.

I and Riya had been seeing each other for more than a year now. And boy I tell you it had been a great year for me. I had cleared my first year in college and come into second year. I had been with a girl that I cared about so much that it made living each day worthwhile. She had given me so many memories that I could live a lifetime with them. I loved her. And she loved me. And we both thought that it was all that we needed. That we could spend our entire life with each other based on that fact. But things had started to go downhill of late. For the past one month we had been fighting almost every day. It had all begun the day after my New Year's disaster. I had fainted and was in the hospital for two days. I had not wished her a happy anniversary. I hadn't told her about my fainting and about being in the hospital for two days. Instead I had told her that I had too much to drink on New Year's so I was knocked out for 24 hours straight.

Although I really had no memories of the time since I fainted to the time I finally recovered consciousness yet a lie was a lie. Did I intend to tell her the truth? Did I want to tell her that I was in the hospital? Had my feeling for her gone with the wind? Did I want to lie to her again and come up with a more believable explanation? Or Did I want to break up with her? Did I not love her anymore?

'Riya' I said and took a pause. It was a long pause. A pause long enough to fit a Karan Johar movie in it. And then finally I spoke.

'I think I love someone else Riya…Her name is Preeti. I have known her for three months now. And yes you are right. I was not that drunk on the day of our Anniversary. I was actually with Preeti at her place. We slept together.' If I was ever in my right mind I would never had said these things. But then maybe I was just not in my right fucking mind. And then what followed was what I deserved for saying that.

'You fucking bastard.' She was literally yelling at me. 'You cheated on me. Oh my god I can't believe it. All this while I kept thinking that maybe I was doing something wrong. But thank god that I now know that it was you all the time. I can't believe I fell in love with someone like you. All my friends used to tell me that I should not be with you. That you would do something like this. But I kept telling them that they were wrong. All you guys are the same. Nothing is more important to you than your bubbling hormones. When your penis speaks all feelings and emotions can go to hell right. All of you think with your dicks too.'

'I am sorry Riya.' I mumbled.

'To fuck with your sorry asshole. We are through. I don't wanna see your fucking face again.'

'Riya......' before I could say anything she hung up on me.

At that moment I realized I had lost someone that meant a hell lot to me. At that moment I figured out that I had lost someone who made me happy. At that moment I knew that what I had done cannot be repaired. That I and Riya will never see each other in the eye again. That Riya would hate me for life. Riya loved me. She loved me more than herself. I meant the world to her. All those moments that we had spent had made me believe that she was the perfect one for me. Then why did I do this to her? Why did I lie to her? Why did I say that I had cheated on her with Preeti? Who was Preeti anyway? Oh ya she was that girl I met at the New Year's party. I hardly knew her. That was the last time I had seen her till then. Nothing had happened between us. Then why did I go ahead and lie to Riya about such a thing? Why was I being such an asshole?

I felt cramped for space. I couldn't breathe. I felt my insides burn. I felt as if my heart was going to explode. I started crying. I picked up the box of cigarettes and lit one. I made my way out of my room puffing on my cigarette. I couldn't stop crying. The image of Riya and all the moments that we had spent together kept flashing me by. I went and knocked on Krish's and Madhur's room. Krish opened the door. I went inside still smoking and poured myself a glass of water. By that time Madhur who was sleeping woke up. Probably my weeping woke him up. They asked me what was wrong and I told them that I and Riya had broken up. They asked me why and I told them over the long distance issue and that I couldn't give her enough time and that is why she had dumped me. Krish and Madhur were my best friends. We had been together for over a year and half. Then why did I have to lie to them too? Why couldn't I just tell them what the truth was? Why couldn't I just tell them what an asshole I had been? Maybe I was scared that they too will give me a piece of their mind. I certainly didn't wanna be alone at this time.

'Let's go to Hotel Sunrise and get drunk.' I said.

'I don't think it's a very good idea.' Krish said.

'Ya Dude I think you should sleep it off. Alcohol will just make you more vulnerable.' Madhur popped in.

'Oh come on. Don't give me any of that vulnerable bullshit. Do you think I can get any more fucking vulnerable? You don't drink if you don't want to. Just for the sake of company. And if I have too much you will have to drive me back.' I think I was just coming to terms with the fact that I and Riya were through and had stopped crying.

'Okay Fine. Let's go.' Krish said.

'And after that we will go and spend the night at Gameplex and play DOTA all night. Tonight I am going to take out all my frustration through that fucking game. I am going to pawn all.' I said.

So anyway I, Krish and Madhur were off to get drunk. I wanted to drown so deep in the spirit of vodka that even Riya herself couldn't pull me back close to her. I wanted to puke out every last bit of Riya from within me. What was done was done and I had to go on with my life because life doesn't wait for anybody. And I was glad that I had my two best pals with me. Without them college wouldn't be half as much fun. Krish and Madhur, two guys whom I hated during my early college days. But today they were my best friends. I would rather die than lose these two guys. At least that is what I thought.

16
FRIENDS WITH BENEFITS

February 2010

'I can't do this.' I said as I backed off but my head hit the cushion on the back seat of my car and I found myself cramped for space with nowhere to go. I looked at the girl who sat on top of me with her each leg on either side of me blocking my exit as she failed to acknowledge what I had just said and put both her arms around my neck and continued drilling my mouth with her tongue. I tried once again as I subtly pushed her back but it didn't help as she started dry-humping me like a deprived nymphomaniac. I finally had to shake her violently to get her to listen what I was saying.

'Stop…please stop. I can't do this.' I said not looking at her.

'Sure you can dude…I know you want me.' It was a rather unexpected response.

'Sorry…but I can't.' I looked up at her with the best puppy face I could make hoping that she would spare me.

'Oh come on get over it dude…Riya and you are over and she's not coming back. So now let's get on with our life….I know this is what you wanted since the day you saw me.' She was really testing my patience now…every second making me more and more angry.

'It's got nothing to do with that.' I said.

'Then what is it. Is this not good enough to turn you on. I can give you head if that will help.' She said and tried to undo my zipper. That was it…she had crossed the line.

'No, that won't help. To tell you the truth I just realized that I don't fancy you at all. I think you are ugly and too fat for my liking. You are one lousy lay.' I lashed out at her.

'Fuck you dude…seriously. I was just doing you a favor to get your mind of that Riya bitch. You should look at yourself…you look like shit. It seems as if she sucked the life out of you and dumped you because she realized that you aren't man enough. You don't have to drop me home…I'll take a cab. You…just go to hell' she got off me, combed her hair and left.

'If this wasn't hell then what is?' I yelled at her disappearing back. She gave me the finger as I saw her get inside a taxi.

I got out of my car that was parked outside The Trident Hotel on Marine Drive and took a walk towards Nariman Point all the time thinking how I had let things come so far.

It was Seema's birthday and she had invited me for her treat at Café Mondegar in Colaba. Seema was a junior of mine in college and over the six months I had known her we had become good friends. There weren't many people who were invited and counting me and

Seema there were six of us. I always loved coming to Café Mondegar. According to me it was the best Café bar in Bombay. I really like the ambience of the place…it is a nice cozy place with a lot of tables placed close to each other. The crowd is almost always excellent. They serve one of the best chicken sausages I have ever had. I love the freshly brewed beer which is served in a down-a-six pitcher. And to top it all, the jukebox has an amazing selection of songs and when something like "Comfortably Numb" or "Hotel California" is played the entire Café full of tipsy heads goes around singing in chorus. This place has never disappointed me when I am looking forward to have a great evening. And it wasn't disappointing today either. We were all having a great time. Since I and Riya broke up I hadn't really gone out a lot…this was my first real outing in a month. And with all the yummy sausages and the beer flowing I was having a good evening. By 11 PM everyone was feeling lightheaded and wanted to call it a day. Neeti was another junior of mine who was going to drop Seema home. Seema although didn't want to go home straight away and asked me what my plans were. I told her that I was driving to Marine Drive and will be sitting there for some time till I got sober so I could drive back like I always did after all my evenings at Café Mondegar. She asked me if I would drop her home if she tagged along and I told her that I would. So after bidding everyone a goodbye Seema and I drove to Marine Drive in my car. We went up to Bachelor's which is an ice cream and juice parlor outside Charni Road station to grab a bite. I ordered a Sandwich and orange juice and Seema ordered a pineapple ice cream as we sat in the car and the waiter got us our order. After eating we drove southwards on Marine

Drive parked the car outside The Trident Hotel and decided to take a walk. We sat down after a while and looked at the vast Arabian Sea in front of us which glittered under the moonlight.

'I'm so sorry for what happened between you and Riya.' Seema said hitting the topic I had dreaded to talk about for a month now. But she continued. 'That is how long distance relationships generally work out...'

'I'm fine *yaar*. And why should you say sorry...it's not like you did anything to break us up. Anyway I don't want to talk about it.' I said cutting her short and making it clear that Riya was one place I didn't want our conversation to go.

'I'm really glad that you came today. I mean after the stories about you Farid has been telling me I had my doubts.' She said hinting at my recently acquired anti-social behavior still not letting go of the topic completely.

'Hmmmm...I'm glad you invited me.' I said as I looked out at the sea avoiding eye contact hoping that at least now she would drop it.

'You know I really like this bearded look of yours' she said.

I looked at her and found her staring at me intently. 'You do? People keep telling me I should shave, every day.' I said as I ran my hand over the beard I had grown...I hadn't shaved in weeks.

'Ya...all of a sudden I think I'm finding you really hot.' she was still staring me down.

'Well...thanks.' I said and a smile crept on my face.

'You know I just have this whole strong feeling of kissing you right now' she said with a very straight face and half open eyes. It felt very weird because her expression certainly did not match up to what she had just said.

'Okay....' Is all I managed to say when she pulled me close to her and started kissing me and biting on my lips like a newly-born-blood-thirsty vampire. I responded by kissing her back which made the moment even more passionate. This is a very sick thing about us guys...if a girl puts the moves on us by herself...we find it almost impossible to turn her down...we are not biologically programmed to turn something like this down...it's beyond our control. No matter what the scenario is...we just walk into it without even giving it a second thought. No wonder girls always say that we think with our dicks...I think to a certain extent it's true.

I and Seema had been kissing for a while now and I guess we were drawing a lot of attention. 'Let's move this someplace more private...your car has tinted windows *na.*' Seema had said. And this was how hell had begun.

Now as I sat at the very end of Nariman Point and looked at the city lights shining I wondered why I had developed cold feet. Why couldn't I do it? It was certainly not because she was ugly...which she was not...she was a little plump but not fat by any standards...I should have just done it I thought. I pondered over Seema's words. She was right...I and Riya were a thing of the past now and she was never coming back. I was feeling horrible and was at an all-time low when my phone rang. The screen said...Preeti Calling. Preeti was the girl I had met at the New Year's bash around two months ago. I had thought that I would never see her again as I had left without even saying a goodbye that night. I wondered for a while why she was calling me and then answered the call on the sixth ring with a huge question mark in my head.

'Hello…' I said.

'….' There came no reply.

'Hello…' I tried again.

'….' Still nothing

'Helloooo…anybody there' I said and still nothing came. I was about to hang up thinking that it was one of those calls that seems to get through when you press the wrong buttons unknowingly when your keypad is not locked when someone tapped me on my right shoulder. I turned around and saw Preeti standing behind me with her phone in her hand.

'I thought it was you…was just confirming.' She said

'Hi…what a pleasant surprise.' I said as I got up to my feet.

'How have you been Aman? Long time no see.' She said getting all friendly…I thought she was a little drunk.

'I have been alright. You tell me…you sound pretty drunk.' I said

'Ya…I was at Café Leopold's with some friends. By the way where did you disappear on New Year's? I couldn't find you anywhere.' She asked.

'*Arre* I had to leave early before the traffic got bad.' I lied. 'So anyway how is Mihir.' I inquired.

'We broke up about a month back. Things just didn't work out after that night and we had to end it.' She told me.

'Awww…that's sad.' I tried to show some sympathy.

'Ya…so how is everything with you…still working on your long distance thing?' I was surprised she remembered that detail.

'Well we too broke up about a month back.' I told her.

'Awww…no wonder you have grown a beard and all. You look like a healthy Jesus.' She smiled.

'Well you don't look that great either you know…you have put on some post break up weight.' I said getting back at her.

'Well that's what I do when I am upset…I eat.' She said.

'And it shows.'

'So tell me what are you doing here all by yourself.' She asked.

'*Arre* I was at Café Mondegar attending a friend's birthday. Just sobering up so that I can drive back.' I told her.

'Oh…so no other plans for the night.' she asked.

'No, none actually.'

'Then maybe you can drop me home…if it isn't too much trouble.'

'Ya sure…no trouble at all.' I said.

I gave Preeti a ride back to her place. We didn't speak much on the way. She kept looking out at the city through her window and told me that she loved the way Bombay looked at night. I knew that as she had told me the same thing on New Year's too. It was around 1.30 AM that I pulled my car outside her building in Worli. She said that we should meet more often and that I should keep in touch. I told her that I will. Then she got out of the car and came over to my side and said goodnight. She started walking towards her building gate and my eyes followed her. Then she stopped, turned around and walked back up to me.

'Hey…if you are not in a hurry then perhaps you can come upstairs for some coffee.' She said. There are two things I have learnt I after watching a lot of Hollywood Romantic Comedy Movies. 1) Never say no to a girl when she ask you to come up for some coffee and 2) When she says Coffee it hardly ever means just coffee.

'Ya sure…that would be lovely.' I said.

And by the time the night got over I had just one thought in my head…Gosh these Hollywood guys really know a lot about girls.

On Sunday the next week Preeti and I decided to meet up for a movie. I had technically avoided all her calls in the week that followed our one night stand and the few calls which I did attend…I just told her that I was keeping busy and I would get back to her once I was free. I guess I was feeling a little guilty about the whole thing that happened and wanted to escape the weird confrontation. But then I realized that escaping wasn't a very mature thing to do and so I agreed to meet her up for the movie. We decided 'My Name Is Khan' as the movie and Globus cinemas Bandra as the venue. Bandra was sort of midway for both of us so it was perfect.

I met Preeti outside Globus Cinemas at 2.30 in the afternoon. We got tickets for the 2.45 show and went inside and took our seats. I was restricting all my answers to mere yes and no in our conversation and was hoping that once the movie started we wouldn't really talk. The movie started after the national anthem and I let myself get carried away with the excellence of SRK's performance.

'So do you wanna talk.' I heard Preeti say. I really hate it when people talk during movies. I mean there is so much brilliance being portrayed on the screen…who really wants to talk. And if you really had to talk why come to the movies…take it to some coffee shop or something.

'You sure wanna talk right now? I heard this movie is excellent.' I said as I kept looking at the 70 mm screen in from of me.

'Aman I have come here all the way from Worli to talk to you. Not to watch this stupid movie.' Okay…now she was calling a SRK movie stupid…this had to be serious.

'Ok fine…what do you wanna talk about.' I said looking at her intently now.

'I wanna talk about us' She said.

'Us?' I said as a bell rang inside my head.

'Yes…us.' She said. The ringing of the bell grew louder.

'Okay fine…I just have to use the rest room and I will be back…okay?' I said.

'Okay.'

I got out of the movie hall and made my way down the corridor. The ringing of the bell was now so loud I felt as if the entire *Durga Puja* from Bengal was happening in my head. Commitment…Commitment…She wants Commitment…a lot of voices were yelling at me. Run…Run…Run as fast as you can…said the others amidst the wild *tandav* which was spooking me out. I didn't really want to use the restroom…I just wanted to run. So I did…I ran…I ran as fast as I could…I ran for my life. I got outside and entered my car turned the ignition on and drove off. I drove off leaving SRK and My Name Is Khan behind me. I drove off leaving

Globus Cinemas and Bandra behind me. I drove off leaving Preeti behind me. I had just gotten out of a relationship and commitment was the last thing I wanted. I just couldn't bear to stand that conversation with Preeti. I felt pathetic that I had to leave her there by herself. I thought she would wait for a while…then look around for a while…and finally understand that I had deserted her. I thought she would call me and hurl some nasty abuses at me…say that she hated me and then I would never hear from her again.

I had driven all the way up till Chembur when I got a text. I pulled my cellphone out of my pocket and checked who it was. It was Preeti. I pulled over my car near a *pan tapri* and got myself a smoke. Then as I realized that I was at a safe distance from Preeti to avoid getting beaten up by her with her sandals I checked out what her text had in store for me. I was ready to go through a lot of slang words but it was nothing of that sort. It read

"Aman I know you are not coming back…and even if you are I won't be there. I'm going out shopping with some friends and will reach home after 10 PM. If by then you are done playing your childish hide and seek games…we can talk like mature adults. Take care :/"

I called up Preeti at 11.30 that night.

'Hi' I said.

'Hi…what's up?' she said sounding totally cool.

'Hey I am sorry about walking out on you like that.' I apologized.

'Ya…it's fine. Don't mention it. Although I felt pretty humiliated but I guess it was obvious that you would do that.' She said.

'Really….why?' I asked

'Because I wanted to talk about us. I know you freaked out and ran for your life.' I was surprised as to how well she understood my pathetic deed.

'Didn't that make you hate me.' I asked.

'Hate…oh no. I have a lot of hatred in my life. I definitely don't want any more of it.' she sounded very calm and continued. 'See…you are misunderstanding me. When I say I want to talk about us I don't mean I want to go out with you or want some kind of commitment from you.'

'You don't?' I asked a little shocked at her words.

'No I don't. See the thing is that I know you have just gotten out of a serious relationship and don't want commitment. I too have been through the same and don't want any commitment myself and that's what I was trying to tell you.' Her words were such a relief.

'Well that's great then.' I said joyfully.

'But here is the deal. What happened between us the other night was great wasn't it.' she asked

'Ya…I guess it was.' I said a little confused.

'Yes it was…and the thing is that it would be a shame if it just turned out to be a one night thing.' There was a long uncomfortable period of silence. She must have realized that I didn't have anything to contribute to the conversation when she laid it out for me word by word. 'See you and me, we are both grown-ups. We have certain needs which have to be fulfilled. Some of them are sexual. So the deal is…only if you are cool with it…that we only see each other to fulfill those needs…you know friends with benefits kinda thing. No feelings…no emotions…no commitments…just sex. What do you say?'

I was at a loss of words. It was all a big surprise for me. Two people being involved with each other over a long time for nothing but sex…the concept was pretty alien to me. But then which guy wants to be tied down. Somewhere within us all guys have a side which just wants to be promiscuous and go around boinking every good looking girl in the universe. Getting all the action without spending time on long phone calls and lousy dates…isn't that just a part of the Bachelor Dream.

'Sounds wonderful.' I said.

17

NOTHING LASTS FOREVER

July 2011

I saw a group of guys standing with their bikes, smoking a few meters away from where I was sitting. They laughed and patted each other…they looked totally engrossed in their conversation. They seemed happy…carefree. I smiled as I saw a shadow of Krish, Madhur and myself in them. 'Innocent buggers' I thought to myself. They didn't have the slightest idea how harsh life could get on them. Then again I stared into infinity. I stared into the infinite depth of that lake which was in front of me. I saw nothing but a reflection of myself. I saw a reflection of me sitting on a cliff all alone looking down at no one but myself. I heard voices…voices that seemed to originate from somewhere deep down inside that lake. They sounded as if someone was talking through a long hollow pipe. I tried to look deeper trying to find out the source of those voices. I found nothing. I thought maybe they were just in my head and tried paying attention to them.

I closed my eyes and I recognized them. They were those laughs and giggles we had shared together. They were those slangs we hurled at each-other on daily basis. I opened my eyes with a start and felt tears creep up in them. Thankfully the voices faded away but then came the vision of everything that had accompanied those voices. The vision of the time when I myself was an innocent carefree bugger. The vision of the time I had friends to call my own. Then came the vision of Krish, Madhur and Aisha.

I had an instant urge to call them and found myself pulling out my phone and dialing Krish's number. Then just as I was going to hit the call button I stopped...I stopped and I had another vision. It was the vision of that night almost one year ago which had changed our life forever. And now as I held on to my phone and saw those memories flash me by for the hundredth time since that day...I felt angry...I felt devastated. I guess it is just one of those psychological things again which makes you wanna destruct when you are angry...anger makes you wanna throw things and break things. I think that was what made me toss my phone into the lake. I sat down after watching my phone drown in the lake with clenched fists and clenched teeth trying to calm down. As I was calming down I wondered about the exact time when these people had started making a difference in my life. I wondered about the time when they actually started mattering to me. I wondered about the time when I had allowed them to become indispensable to me. I couldn't really think of a particular time or place. But then I guess it's all a part of a process. A process of knowing someone...accepting someone... befriending someone... liking someone. It is all a long complex process…Loving someone and Hating someone…It's all just a process.

Bombay Rains 2010

It was Krish's birthday and he threw a party at Indulge Lounge in Belapur. The party had begun and was in full flow when I made my entrance.

'*Bhenchod…* you are late.' I found a slightly drunk Krish come over to me.

'Dude I was a little caught up.' I said. Krish looked at me apprehensively. 'What ?' I asked

'You were playing DOTA weren't you. Bastard you were playing DOTA.' He had got me. I think it's just that we both knew each other so well that it was impossible to hide anything. But this wasn't great…I had to come up with something better. After all I had shown up at his party three hours late conveniently.

'No dude I wasn't…it was something else.' I said still trying to think of some good excuse which would get me off the hook.

'What something else?' he asked

'I think it is best not to talk about it.' I said as I still couldn't think of a good enough excuse.

'Aman you crazy bastard…you turn up for my…your best friend's birthday party three hours late and you say there was something keeping you a little caught up. And then you say you don't wanna talk about it. What the fuck is wrong with you.' I think he had already downed a lot alcohol which was making him behave this way. I mean what ever happened to giving each-other their own space. I even considered telling him that but then realized…that the line only works with extremely clingy girlfriends and intruding Pinocchio nosed relatives. But as he went on about how he wouldn't let me go without knowing why I was late a light bulb glowed in my head.

'It's Riya.' I said 'Riya had called' I lied through my teeth.

'Oh….Oh…okay…is everything fine.' He looked a little uncomfortable and I knew I had got my man. He had seen me in a chronic state of a nervous breakdown after my break up with Riya. I guess ever since I told him about my arrangement with Preeti he always thought that Riya had managed to get the dark side of me out in the open. Riya was a territory which was out of bounds and was never ever to be discussed.

'Ya I'm fine.' I said.

'Great then…don't spoil your mood and enjoy the party.' He said and led me towards the bar.

It was a great party. Almost half my class was invited. I chatted up with everyone and was having a good time. The alcohol kept flowing in and within no time I started feeling light headed. I have this rule which I have made about drinking in pubs and lounges. It is that if you have too much to drink in such places you should start dancing. It helps you sober up and creates room for more.

So I danced…I danced like there was no tomorrow. My world was spinning and I could hear all my classmates cheer me up. I felt great. After a while I went up to the bar again to get myself a beer. I found Disha there. Disha was my classmate…she was an NRI. She stayed in Seattle. If I had to describe her the words tall, dusky and attractive would never cross my mind. But today she did look unbelievably attractive.

'Hey…how are you?' She said as I took the seat next to her.

'I am good…how are you?' I asked.

'Oh I am fine…What's up with you lately? Haven't really seen you around.' She said as she took a sip from her drink which I think was Bloody Mary.

'Well nothing much has been up. I have been a little cut off from the world.' I regretted saying this as soon as I said it and hoped she would not bring up the same goddamn topic again.

'Ya I heard. Aisha told me.' She said. Disha and Aisha were best friends so I wasn't surprised that she knew. I was actually glad because I was spared from telling the story all over again. 'So then…what's new apart from your whole anti-social stint? Back out there?' she asked

'Back out where?' I asked only half listening to her as I was trying hard to get the bartender's attention. He finally acknowledged me and got me the beer. I took a sip and looked back at Disha 'Ya…you were saying?' I asked.

'Are you seeing someone?' She asked

'Don't you think it's a little too soon?' I said. 'And anyway I think I'm done with all this dating business…it's a lot of *jhol*. I think I am better off by keeping things simple.' I said and gulped some more beer.

'You mean like a one night stand.' She asked wryly. I smiled

'Ya like a one night stand.' I said.

'So do you see any targets out here that might fall prey to your dimpled boyish charms.' I could sense the flirt meter in her rise.

'You might.' I said calmly and sipped my beer. She looked at me as if I had just told her that I was Osama Bin Laden. 'Just kidding' I said and allowed her room to breathe. 'See the point is...half of the chicks out here are so drunk that they are easy targets to pick up. But by the time we get back to their place they will be so sloshed they will pass out in front of me. Then it just becomes a one night sit...Which is just pathetic.' I explained to her.

'You really sound as if you have been doing a lot of picking up lately.' She said.

'Well it's either that or the fact that I follow *How I Met Your Mother* religiously.' I smiled back at her.

I saw Aisha walk towards me as I finished my beer.

'There you are Mr.Smarty Pants...I have been looking for you everywhere.' She said. I realized I had met up with everyone except Aisha that night.

'Well you know where to find me at a party...it's either here or on the dance floor.' I said. She looked at me and pouted.

'I never really understand this guy.' She told Disha. 'He is this crazy fellow who does all weird things in life. I don't know why I am friends with him.' Disha just smiled and looked at me. Aisha continued 'I have to talk to you mister...you never even bother returning my calls...and I haven't seen you in ages.'

'Okay fine...talk.' I said as I got ready to listen to one of those long grandmotherly lectures that Aisha generally has in store for me. She is always full of that agony aunt bullshit.

'I will after a while…right now everyone on the dance floor is missing you so you have to come with me.' She said pulling on my arm.

'I will come only if you dance with me.' I said trying hard to resist.

'Ya fine…now come.' She dragged me.

I hit the dance floor with a vengeance and tried to blur of the world in front of me. But the DJ was keen on making things turn ugly. He played the song '*Kahin toh hogi woh*' from *Jaane tu Ya Jaane Na*. That was my special song for Aisha. I had seen that movie with her and every time it played I had an instant urge to hold Aisha and never let her go. I knew it was a pathetic thought…she was my best friend's girlfriend after all. To make matters worse Aisha had come close to me and we were slow dancing together. I felt a chill go down my spine and as she put her hand on my shoulder and moved her cheek next to mine. As I have already said before…Aisha was the most beautiful girl I had ever known. Male mind I tell you…it is god's worst creation.

'I remember you told me once that this song reminds you of me.' Aisha said as she looked at me deeply. I nodded. 'It is a lovely song. I feel so nice dancing with you…reminds me of those good old days when you were such a sweetheart. What ever happened to that Aman? Why have you been behaving like a total ass up late.' She said as she rested her head on my shoulder.

In that moment I wanted to hold her and kiss her…instead I let go of her and made my way towards the balcony. Fresh air…I needed some fresh air. I lit up a cigarette and puffed on it as I looked at the cars pass by on the road below. Aisha came looking for me a few moments later.

'What's wrong Aman.' She asked.

'Go away.' I said not looking at her.

'No I won't go away…not unless you tell me what's wrong.' She said. I didn't care to respond. She moved in next to me. 'What is bothering you? Why have you been so off lately?' she asked

'Aisha…listen…I am in no mood to talk okay. Just leave me alone.' I said.

'What the hell is your problem. I know you have been through a bad break up but that is a part and parcel of life. You just have to let it go and move on with your life. Life is not easy Aman…it never was and never will be. You can't just run away from everything you know. This thing of locking yourself up and being all anti-social, it is bad. It is bad for you and for the people who care about you. And what is this thing I heard about Preeti and you. Have you lost it. Friends with benefits…are you completely out of your mind. Sleeping with random chicks is not going to help achieve anything. Aman…Aman…are you even listening to what I'm saying.' She was really poking at the wrong buttons.

'Ya whatever.' I said and hoped she would just leave me alone.

'What ya whatever…come on stop being this way. This doesn't suit you. Embrace the life God has given you and be grateful for it.

Come on now stop being an ass and come inside.' She said and tried to pull me inside.

'Leave me alone Aisha. For god sake just leave me alone.' I blasted at her.

'Why are you being so difficult Aman.' She asked a little taken aback by my outburst.

My anger level was at its peak 'Oh I am sorry Aisha…I'm sorry for being difficult…I'm sorry for being an ass…I'm sorry for not being the sweetheart dimple cheeked Aman that you call your friend. For all you know that Aman died. And you think you know a lot about life because you are always being an agony aunt to everyone. But here is a newsflash for you. Not everyone's life is as perfect as yours. Not everyone's life is happy as yours is. All these words about embracing life and all…are all bullshit. You think you know a lot about my life because you hear stuff from Krish. *Arre* even Krish knows nothing about me. He calls me his best friend but the truth is I know everything about him and he knows nothing about me. No one knows anything. You and Krish have been living a life which is a cakewalk. No issues to deal with…no complications. Sorry to burst your happy bubble but I know you will too come across a time when your world will be devastated…and Krish won't be there to comfort you.' I erupted like a violent volcano.

'How dare you…you think I don't have my problems?…you think it's just you who has a complicated life?…Do you have any idea as to how much we cry thinking about the day when college gets over? I'm a Muslim and my parents would never allow me and Krish to be together. But we never let it affect what we have between us. I love him and he loves me and that is all that matters. You bloody call him your best friend and say you know everything about him...now tell me do you? I know I'm living in a dream which is going to come to a horrid end someday. But that doesn't stop me from living it today. I was just trying to help you to realize the same thing.' She said as tears rolled down her eyes.

Generally a crying girl would melt my heart but I don't know what was wrong with me today. Her tears didn't have any effect on me...instead I blasted out at her. 'You know what...Fuck you and your help. I don't want any of it. I'm not looking for anyone's sympathy. So shove it and leave me alone.'

I saw Aisha go inside with tears in her eyes and knew what was coming. I lit up another cigarette and waited for it patiently. It came around ten minutes later. I could sense it. I turned around and saw Krish and Madhur standing behind me.

'What happened?' Madhur asked.

'What do you mean what happened?' I asked looking at Krish who was standing quietly.

'Aisha came in crying after talking to you...so what happened?' Madhur rephrased his question.

'Why don't you ask her?' I said and turned around.

'*Behenchod* you listen to me...tell me what happened or...' Krish said fuming.

'Or what...you'll hit me...go on...hit me.' I said staring him down.

'Bastard just tell me what you said.' He said as if he meant business.

'Fine if you must know…your pain in the ass girlfriend wanted to meddle with my life so I asked her to go fuck herself and leave me alone.' I said.

'You said what?' He asked again.

'What are you…deaf or something…I told your slut of a girlfriend to leave me…' was all I could say when out of nowhere Krish's hand came down smacking on my face. I looked back at him and at Madhur and then at all my classmates who had gathered at the balcony entrance to see the show.

'You pathetic son of a bitch…how the fuck can you say such a thing about her. She thinks so highly of you and you repay her with this. If not her at least you could have thought about me and our friendship you asshole.' Krish said as he looked at me with pity in his eyes.

'Are you done?' I asked him and then without waiting for his reply I stormed out of the balcony and out of the lounge. Got in my car and drove down Palm Beach Road like a maniac who was out to kill and get killed. I didn't come back to the hostel that night. I knew there would be a lot of questions asked and I won't have the answers. I drove all the way to Worli to meet Preeti after grabbing a bottle of Vodka from the wine shop on the way. I finished half of the bottle while driving. The last thing I remember was ringing her door bell as I passed out.

The next day Preeti woke me up. She had made some coffee. My head was hurting like it had never hurt before. The memories of last night were still fresh. I checked my phone and there were fifteen missed calls, ten from Madhur…one from Krish…one from Aisha and two from home. Preeti asked me what had happened last night and I told her that I and Krish had got into a major fight and basically our friendship was over. Madhur called me after a while and I answered.

'Hey where the fuck are you? You didn't come back last night we were so worried?' he said.

'How does it matter. I'm not dead…and if I do die…you'll get the invitation for the funeral.' I said.

'What is wrong with you Aman…why are you being so obnoxious?' he asked.

'Oh now I have to ask for your permission to behave obnoxiously.' I said.

'Aman listen…what Krish did last night was uncalled for…but what you did was wrong…he is worried about you and so is Aisha…just come back and talk it out…it'll be fine.' Madhur said like a man on a mission.

'See Madhur…I don't wanna talk anything out…from now on I don't give a damn about Krish or Aisha. They don't exist for me. And you stop telling me what to do alright.' I said making it clear that I did not want any reconciliation.

'But this is not good…just apologize and everything will be as it was.' He said.

'I'm not apologizing to anyone…I have done nothing.' I said

'Oh so you think…calling Aisha what you called her was nothing.' Madhur said.

'You know what...I don't have to listen to all this bull crap from you...I'm hanging up...you go and lick Krish's ass like you always do...bye' I said as I hung up.

I knew what happened that day would never be forgotten. From being best friends for life we turned into mere shadows of ourselves who crossed each-other's path everyday but never as much looked at each-other. I felt horrible but as they say...time heals all wounds. They moved on with their life and I moved on with mine.

18
HEY...IT'S MY BIRTHDAY... ☹

September 2010

The last couple of months had been tough on me...actually they had been a disaster. There was nothing that made me thrive forward. An untimely break up with a girl whom I loved...a huge spat with my friends who mattered to me more than anything...so to sum it up...my life was a complete mess. If I have to compare it to anything then it would surely be the Lost City Of Atlantis...in ruins with all the glory behind it...submerged in the depth of unknown waters. In my case...I was more or less submerged into huge quantities of alcohol and the empty, hollow thoughts.

I would often take long walks by myself to nowhere until I realized how far I actually was or how late it was getting. There was this one day I found myself sitting in a train at the Victoria Terminal as people rushed past me to get off it. It takes around one, one and a half hour to reach VT from my place by train. But I had no memories of anything that might have happened in that time…I didn't know why I took the train to VT in the first place. I thought a lot about my life sitting down on the foot path near the Times Of India office as I saw Bombay move at the its rapid pace right in front of me. Sitting there in the evening all jobless I looked at those speeding vehicles…I saw those corporate executives rushing home to their wives, girlfriends and friends…I saw young college guys hitting the bars…I saw couples walking hand in hand…I saw hookers getting picked up…I looked at the neon lights shining on the billboards which had the faces of huge celebrities on them. All this really made me feel small…Bombay made me feel small. All my life the only thing I ever wanted was to become that man who was looking at me from the huge Tag Heuer billboard. And now as I sat in front of my idol and looked at him…Bombay was passing me by without even noticing me. I guess that is what happens to people when they start believing that they are special…the world comes crashing down on them. I think it is a way in which the almighty tells you… 'Hey…you fool…you think you are special huh? …Now suck on this.' Well whatever it is…it hurts…it hurts like someone has stabbed you with a knife and then just to torture you he is rotating the knife inside your body. You want to cry and beg for it stop…but it doesn't…it goes on till the time you stop feeling anything or till the time you die. I sat there for hours with my head in my hands…crying…thinking what went wrong…and then crying some more.

'Dude that's my spot.' I looked up at the guy who was standing next to me. He was old and wore tattered clothes. He was carrying a stick and had dark goggles on. 'Get out of here and find your own spot or I'll hit you.' He said. It took me some time to figure out that I was invading the territory of a beggar and he was shooing me away.

I was in my room listening to some music, crying and boozing the night away when I got a call. It was Mom. I checked out what time it was…it was forty minutes past midnight. Why was mom calling me up so late? I picked up.

'Hello.' I said.

'Hello *beta*.' Came the reply.

'Hi Mom…what's up?' I said in a sad depressed voice.

'Aman…what are you doing?' Mom asked

'Nothing Mom just sitting in my room.' I said as I wiped my tears.

'Are you okay? Have you been crying?' she asked. How do Moms know everything…it is just unreal.

'No Mom…I'm fine. You tell me…how come you called.' I asked

'To wish you a Happy Birthday *beta* why else…what is wrong with you Aman?' she said. OH Fuck…I thought to myself…I had forgotten my own birthday…what the fuck was wrong with me. Nobody had called to wish me…every year I got so many calls right from midnight that it was impossible to forget the fact that it was my birthday. But this year there was nothing…not even a text so far. It felt horrible…I thought I would start crying again.

'Nothing is wrong…and thank you for calling.' I said trying hard to suppress my emotions.

'Aman…tell me what happened? Why are you not celebrating with your friends?' Mom asked in a stern voice. Gosh I missed her. I missed her so much...all I really wanted was to be with her...I wanted to rest my head in her lap and cry like a little child who gets bullied in school. Well I was being bullied...I was being bullied by life.

'Mom...I love you.' I said and surpassed the emotional barrier as tears came flooding back in my eyes. 'I love you Mom.'

'I love you too *beta*. Are you okay...I think you should come back home.' she said.

'No Mom...not now...I still have a lot of work here...and plus exams are coming...I will be back soon.' I said.

'What can possibly be so important that you can't even celebrate your birthday? Just come back...to hell with exams...they don't matter. We will go on a nice long vacation to Europe.' Her voice had grown soft and I could hear her sob softly.

'Mom...don't worry...I'm fine. I will come back soon...I promise.' I said

'How can I not worry *beta*...you are so far away from us...I miss you so much.' She said as the emotions got the better of her.

'Don't cry Mom...I am fine...I miss you too...don't cry. I love you *na.*' it always hurts when I see my Mom crying.

'I love you too *beta*. You take care of yourself okay...and tell me if you feel like coming back.' She said.

'I will Mom...take care...goodnight.' I said as I hung up the phone. Why was life being so hard on me. Why couldn't I just have a normal life...why the fuck were things this way? I couldn't even feel good on my birthday. It is the one day of the year on which not even Sad Joe is supposed to be depressed. And here I was feeling rejected and deserted on my own freaking birthday.

I logged onto my Facebook page to check out if anyone had bothered to wish me. There were some fifty notifications. Out of the six hundred odd friends in my friend list, fifty of them had wished me...well that brought some relief. I checked out all my wall posts and replied to each of them personally. I would never have done that if this was any other birthday...instead I would have just updated my status saying... 'Thank you everyone for wishing me. God Bless you all.' ...Without even meaning it. But I guess it is only when you are at your all time low you realize the worth of being humble. Today when I had no friends to call my own...these fifty people for whom I never gave a shit seemed to mean more than anything. I was just going to log off when a chat window popped up. It was Preeti.

Preeti : Hey...Happy Birthday.

Aman : Hey...Thanks a ton ☺

Preeti : So...where is the party?

Aman : No party *yaar* ☺

Preeti : Why what's wrong?

Aman : No one to party with. ☺

Preeti : You are still not talking to the guys?

Aman : Nope.

Preeti : They must have wished you *na?*

Aman : Nope. Not a word since that day.

Preeti : That is just sad ☺ What the fuck did you do?

Aman : Forget it *yaar.* I don't wanna talk about it.

Preeti : Ok fine...so what else?

Aman : Nothing much...just sitting in my room listening to music and drinking.

Preeti : Drinking...all by yourself?

Aman : Yup.

Preeti : That is a very sad way to celebrate your birthday ☺

Aman : Can't help it...can I?

Preeti : Well if you want...we can meet up. You can treat me if you like ☺

Aman: Well actually that doesn't sound so bad *wink* I can treat you with a special something...hehe.

Preeti : Gosh...you and your perverted mind *wink*

Aman : Hey don't blame it on me...you were the one who started it ☺

Preeti : Ya whatever...where do you wanna go?

Aman : How about The Hard Rock Café?

Preeti : Ya...sounds good. What time?

Aman : Around 9 in the evening?

Preeti : Okay cool.

Aman : Fine...I'll see you then.

Preeti : Okay...*chal* anyway I gotta sleep now. Goodnight and Take care.

Aman : Goodnight...Bye.

Well this wasn't so bad...at least I had a date for my birthday. I gulped down the remaining vodka and went into the state of trance which was triggered by Armin Van Buren and "The Light Between Us." I slept like a baby.

I met Preeti at The Hard Rock Café in Parel around nine thirty. The place was jam packed with people which wasn't surprising as it was a Saturday. We couldn't find a table for ourselves so we decided to order at the bar. The atmosphere was electrifying like it always is. The Hard Rock Café in Mumbai is one place where till today I have never found a table to sit…but that has never stopped me from having a great time. The music is always great and the ambience is nothing less than that of a live concert. We were having a good time and after having a couple of drinks nothing seemed to matter…all our inhibitions disappeared. We were now singing the songs out loud and were head banging to the rocking tunes. After having five Martini's Preeti went nuts…she pulled in a lot of people and gathered them together around us.

'Hello everyone.' She said. 'My name is Preeti and this is my friend Aman. Today I am very happy…and you know why…because it is his birthday. It is his fucking birthday and I have a big surprise for him…which I won't tell you. Everyone enjoy.' She was drunk and out of her senses. I didn't care much as I was not very sober myself. Everyone started wishing me and congratulating me and in that crowd I lost Preeti. Then after a while I heard her voice again on the speakers. I looked up at the DJ console and found her there with the microphone in her hand.

'Aman Sarin…will you please come up here. Aman Sarin come up here.' She said. Well I thought this was going to be one of the most embarrassing moments of my life but still I made my way up to the console. 'This is my friend Aman…he is not my boyfriend…we are just friends…do you get what I mean.' She said.

'Nooooooo' replied the crowd. What the hell was she doing I thought. I found out soon.

'We are fuck buddies.' She said and the crowd roared and applauded. 'So if any girls think that he is hot…feel free to pounce on him…and it is his birthday today…so please wish him.'

I stood there in a state of shock as the crowd cheered 'Happy birthdayyyyy.' And then she pulled herself close to me and planted a huge kiss on my lips.

Gosh that was embarrassing. I made my way back to the bar with Preeti and got back to drinking trying to avoid all contact with the people around me. This was definitely the most embarrassing moment of my life. I could feel it…I could feel that somewhere people were looking at me and laughing their asses off. I was finishing my peg of Vodka-Tonic when Preeti came over.

'Will you walk me to the wash room? I think I am too drunk to walk on my own.' She said

'Ya sure.' I said as I walked with her towards the ladies room.

'Please wait here for a while.' She said as she entered the loo. I stood there for around five minutes waiting for her to come out. She peeped out of the door and looked around and then pulled me into the ladies room with her.

'Preeti…What the fuck? …are you mad.' I said as I tried to exit.

'This is your surprise' she said and pinned me against the door and locked it. We made out in ladies room and it was amazing.

We took a cab back to her place as I was in no condition to drive. It had been a wild night and things got wilder in the bedroom. We didn't make love…it was not something you can put under the category of making love. It was sex…wild passionate sex. We were like animals in bed following our instincts. We carried on till both of us were spent and exhausted. I slept in at her place that night.

The next day I woke up to find Preeti out of bed. I put on my clothes and walked out to living room. She was in the kitchen. She had a long shirt on and wore nothing under it. I went up to her and put my hands around her.

'Hey…good morning.' I said and kissed her on her neck.

'Hey…did you sleep okay.' She said and turned to face me.

'Like a log.' I said.

'Good. So what do you want for breakfast?' She asked.

'What are you making?' I asked and nibbled on her lips.

'Toast and omelets.' She said and looked at me like a doll.

'That will do. I will make some coffee. You want?' I said and made my way towards the electric kettle in the dining room.

'Ya sure.' She said. I was reading the newspaper while heating the water when she called out from the kitchen. 'Last night was good.'

'Good…naaa…it was awesome baby.' I said

'Aman…I'm sorry if I embarrassed you at Hard Rock. I was so drunk.' She said as she got our breakfast to the dining table.

'Don't be silly Preeti…it's fine…it's not like I'm going to meet anyone from there daily. I had a lot of fun and that is what matters' I said sincerely

'I had a great time too…thank you for taking me.' She said.

'Are you crazy…I should thank you…if it wasn't for you I would have been all alone celebrating a shitty birthday.' I kissed her on the cheek and took a seat next to her.

'So what are your plans for today?' she asked.

'Well nothing specific. I have to pick my car from Hard Rock and then nothing… I will go back to the hostel and sit in my room watch some movies…the usual. Do you have anything in mind?' I said

'Ya actually I too have no plans…and today is Sunday so I was thinking if you would like to stay in with me.' She said.

'I would love to.' I said

'Ya?' she asked.

'Yup…why not?' I said and took a sip of my coffee.

'Okay great…we will watch some good movies and then go out in the evening for dinner…we can pick up your car then.' She said.

But we did not pick up my car in the evening. We did not even go out to get dinner. I cooked some pasta for lunch and we baked two pizzas for dinner. We spent the entire afternoon after lunch cuddling on the sofa watching "Love and Other Drugs" and then the entire evening before dinner pretending as if she was Anne Hatheway and I was Jake Gyllenhal in the bedroom. After dinner we did the dishes together and retired back into our love den. What a birthday weekend it was turning out to be. It was definitely not the worst as I had expected. I was ready to spend another night at her place… we were lying next to each-other when she threw the blockbuster of the week at me.

'Aman…do you think you can move in with me?' She asked. It caught me completely off guard. I wasn't expecting this.

'I don't know. I mean it's a huge step and my college is quite far from here.' I said.

'*Arre* not here…we will get our own place somewhere midway.' She said.

'Well can I think about this…I mean I need sometime? My exams are coming so maybe after that.' I said.

'Ya sure…take your time.' She said and turned the other way. I got her signal.

'I will see you soon.' I said as I turned the lights off and made my way out of her apartment. I picked up my car and drove back to Nerul…all the while thinking about Preeti's proposal. Were we getting serious about each other? Was she falling in love with me? Was I falling in love with her? All these questions didn't seem to matter. There was just one question which surpassed all others… Why Me God…Why Me?

19
DAD...I MADE YOU PROUD

November 2010

The prelim exams were now a thing of the past. They had come and rocked me like a hurricane. I had failed miserably in all the four subjects of second year MBBS. My internal marks were screwed as a result of my poor performance. Terming my performance as poor will definitely be an understatement...it was pathetic...hopeless. I had just managed to score 6 on 20 in Pharmacology...5 on 20 in Pathology...10 on 20 in Microbiology and 5 on 10 in Forensic Medicine. It was most certainly a time when I had to do a reality check and set my priorities right.

The final University exams came knocking shortly and I sank myself in those big piles of paper they call books. But no matter how hard I tried to study...no matter how hard I tried to concentrate...my thoughts always went wandering to the happenings of the last couple of months. Ever since I had joined college I had never studied alone.

Krish, Madhur and I had developed a great chemistry between ourselves which allowed us to study together and bring out the best from us. We used to keep testing each other's knowledge with the toughest of questions which made us work harder. I did not know a way to study without them around me. And the fact that both Krish and Madhur had managed to ace the prelim exam only made things harder. I kept thinking that weren't they affected by what had happened between us…didn't the whole thing bother them at all. Preeti had asked me to move in with her. That was another thought that kept me occupied for hours together. The way things were going I was sure I was heading for an ATKT in three subjects if I was lucky. In the worst case scenario I would flunk all the four subjects and receive six months back.

Desperate times called for desperate measures and I took them. I undertook the time tested formula of Lie, Cheat and Steal. I lied to my parents about my prelim's result. I cheated in exams like it was the only thing I knew. And I stole…I stole the question papers. Yes that is true…well I did not steal them myself…but I bribed a lot of people, from peons to professors to get the job done.

When exams came I had all the question papers of all the subjects right in front of me a night before they started. There was a lot of work still to be done. Having the question paper doesn't necessarily mean that you will pass. You have to know the answers to them too. I took the easy way out here as well. Chits…a lot of chits with all the answers written down on them was all it took to make exams look like a joy ride.

The results came out two weeks later. I got a distinction in all the four subjects. It was not just the distinctions…I had topped the class. I remember a lot of people giving me cold stares the day I went to check my result. 'How the fuck did this guy top?' was the question running in their heads which was pretty evident from their facial expressions. Seeing my name on the top of the list didn't really make me happy. As a matter of fact I felt sorry for myself. If leaking question papers was what it took for me to top then it was certainly not something I wanted to do. I didn't really care for the rank…all I wanted to do was pass the exam. There were a lot of people who had worked their asses off throughout the year to achieve what I had achieved by shelling out a few bucks. I wanted to go and tell them about my dark reality. I wanted to tell them that they were the ones who were the real winners and I was just some fucking loser who had leaked the papers. And I proved that to myself when I decided to remain quiet instead of owning up my fraud. I called up Dad that night to inform him the result.

'We are so proud of you son. You have no idea how much we worry about you every day. We keep thinking that someday this world would get the better of you and pray against it. And every time you come out strong and prove us and the world wrong. I and your mother are very proud that you are our son…we love you.' My Dad said after I told him that I had topped the class.

I wanted to tell him that he was wrong. I wanted to tell him that the world had not just gotten the best of me but had broken me down to small tiny pieces which I could not fix back. I wanted to tell him what I had done and how I had topped the class. I wanted to say that I was nothing but a coward and they should be ashamed of me.

But the way he had said his words made it impossible for me to own up to him. His words were a mix of pride, care, happiness and love…something which I had rarely received from Dad. It brought back all those memories of the days when I had let him down… The days when I had emerged second in place of first as he had expected. I remembered the day when I had told him that I didn't want to become a doctor…I remembered the disappointment in his eyes as he walked away from me without even saying a word.

I had hurt my Dad a lot in the past and listening to him happy was all that seemed to matter at that time. Call me a loser…call me a coward…call me whatever you want to but there was no way I was telling him the truth. All I wanted was him to be happy and now that he was, even leaking papers to top the exam didn't seem that bad.

'I love you too Dad.' Was all that I could say.

20
SELF-DESTRUCTION MODE - ON

December 2010

There was a new found hatred for me in college. Everywhere I went I could sense people giving me weird looks and having some conversation among themselves. The days when people saw me in college and acknowledged me, greeted me and chatted up with me now seemed long gone. They were now replaced by days where people would conveniently ignore me after looking at me. The word about my tiff with Krish on his birthday had spread like wildfire. The whole topic...that something which had made Krish and me...who were inseparable...draw apart... seemed like the scoop of the century. It was hot and juicy gossip material. People made up their own stories. Everyone had a different take on it. Some said that I showing up late for his party had led to it. Some said that I had abused him after getting drunk. The others said that I was hitting on Aisha. There were a few who even went to the extent of saying that I had been sleeping with Aisha behind Krish's back. Whatever the story was…I was the bad guy in all of them. All this with the fact that a chronic bunker like me had topped the University exams made them develop platonic hatred for me. Things were not just restricted to college…back in the hostel as well I had become someone who had betrayed a fellow hosteller. I was seemingly being boycotted by each and every person living in the hostel. I even found my name scribbled on some walls with nasty abuses suffixed in front of it. Hostel had definitely become a hostile place to stay.

In mid-December I moved out of the hostel and rented a place outside college. I told Preeti about my plans of shifting out a few days before I did shift. She brought up the topic of moving in together again. It took me over an hour to convince her that the whole thing was a little impractical and not very convenient for both of us. She said she understood…and I really hoped that she did. She offered to help me move in to my new place and I accepted.

The place that I had rented was in Sector 19 Nerul. It was a duplex row house and was situated in a very quiet residential area. There was a small temple and a *gurudwara* right next to my house and a small park behind it. The whole feel of the place was very peaceful. It had a terrace which overlooked the park which made it the perfect place for me. I really needed to organize my thoughts and sort my life and with all the serenity and peace this place seemed to provide I had to take it. Preeti helped me with the shifting…there really wasn't much help which was needed…I only had a three bags the rest of the stuff like the AC, the mattress, the cupboard etc was moved in by professional packers and shifters. But I think she liked hanging out with me and I too liked having her around. She helped me unpack my clothes and arranged them properly in my cupboard. She spread out the bed covers and folded my blanket and made my bed all perfect. We put on the curtains together and arranged my table. We went grocery shopping and she picked out stuff which was very important and I didn't know existed. She did everything with so much enthusiasm that for a moment I thought that maybe we were moving in together.

By the time she was done...the place seemed like home. A neat room, a well-made bed, fridge full of stuff, furniture laid our properly... it was a feeling that I had missed for a long time. In the evening I opened a bottle of white wine we had brought and poured out two glasses of it. We sat on the terrace sipping our wine as we saw the sun setting down at the far horizon behind the concrete forest. There were small kids who were playing on the swings and the slides in the park in front of us...health conscious fat middle aged aunties taking their evening walks... young couples hopelessly in love enjoying time with each other behind the trees. That evening everyone seemed happy. Even I was happy...I was happy that I had shifted out of the hostel...I was happy that now I had a place to call my own...I was happy to be with Preeti. I hadn't felt this way in a long time and this was really a welcome change. I guess happiness is just a state of mind than a feeling. Even when your life is in a complete turmoil and nothing seems to be right...there are some things which just make you feel happy...they take your mind off things which you are struggling with everyday...sometimes such happiness seems to over throw any other kind of joy you might have experienced.

After finishing our wines we went down to my room and I put on some music. Music is another thing which can have a hell of an impact on your state of mind… for me music definitely sets the mood. I was lying down on my bed and Preeti was checking her mail on my laptop…I don't have a clue when I got carried away with the sound of Enigma and got lulled in a sweet sleep. When I woke up late at night the lights were turned off and Preeti was gone. She had removed my specs and put them away…she had put a pillow under my head and tucked me in with a blanket over me. The music was still playing. I found a note on my table…it said…

"Gone Home – Preeti."

I felt bad…I hadn't even thanked her for all her help…the least I could have done was drive her back. I texted her immediately…

'Hey…Thanks for everything Preeti…I don't know what I would have done without you…thank you so much for making my home. And sorry for just sleeping off…I would have driven you back…Thanks again.'

Her reply came a few minutes later

'Anytime sweetheart…anytime.'

Living by myself allowed me to have a lot of free time for myself. I spent most of the time listening to music and analyzing my life. My biological cycle had reversed itself. I spent majority of my time in the day sleeping and I spent the nights wide awake. When you are alone and have nothing to do…there is always one thing which never fails to amuse you…alcohol. And I was consuming huge quantities of it. I used to buy different stuff everyday…some days I had beer…some days vodka…some days rum. I was turning into an ideal alcoholic. Things got worse and living without alcohol seemed impossible.

I would get up late in the evening…go to the liquor store and buy what I wanted…then I would get some food parceled…after that began a long night for me, my alcohol, my songs and my thoughts. I would generally sit on the terrace as I got drunk. Preeti would come over frequently and we would have some wild sex. Sex…that was all that it meant to me now. It was just a physical need which had to be fulfilled. There was no emotion attached to it. We would just do it like two dogs in heat and that was just about it. Soon even that ended and things became cold. Like Paulo Cohelo had described in his book…the sex was now only as good as those ELEVEN MINUTES.

'Why do you drink so much?' Preeti asked me one night.

'Because that is the only way I know how to live anymore.' I said

'You know…you can seriously die if you don't stop.' She said.

'And you know…I can seriously die anyway.' I laughed.

'Aman…I am serious. I really can't see you this way.' She had a lot of concern in her voice.

'And you know what Preeti…this is the only way I want to be.' I said as I peered deep into her eyes.

'Aman come on *yaar*…you haven't gotten out of this place ever since you shifted…let's go out somewhere.' She said as she tried to pull me up to my feet.

'No *yaar*… you go. I have been out there and done everything that is to be done. And I think there is no better place than this place.' I said

'You know what…I think you are impossible…this fight that you had with Krish and Madhur has really taken its toll on you. I think you should talk to them and sort things out…you'll feel better.' She said.

'I don't wanna talk to them…and don't you fucking start up on that topic…it's none of your business.' I lashed out at her.

'That's right…it's not my business…even you are not my business. I am not your girlfriend after all…you are so difficult Aman. And you have no regard for the people who care for you…no wonder the guys…' she said and I cut her short.

'Enough.' I said.

'That's it.' she said after a few seconds. 'You don't' have anything else to say?'

I remained silent and finished the vodka in my glass in one large sip.

'Great…now you wanna give me silent treatment. Well I am going anyway. I was just here to take you to this show in the Marriot. SRK is going to be there and I thought you would be interested…but I guess now all you care about is yourself…bye…see you later.' She said and left.

I heard the door being shut downstairs. I sat down and pondered over Preeti's words. Why were all girls so complicated. If she had to take me to the show…she should have just said so. I would have jumped to the thought of meeting SRK…what was she trying to do…was she trying to make me realize that she was doing a favor for me. And what was with all that talk about Krish and Madhur. Whatever it was I had blown away my chance of meeting SRK…the man I looked up to. The days had passed by and my dream of being the next big thing in Bollywood had remained just a dream. Now when I thought of it…it wasn't even a dream anymore. It was just a stupid thought which was knocked out of my head by the stark reality. All these thoughts made me hurt and I tried to numb them as I put my mouth on the bottle of vodka and gulped down all of it in one go. I think I puked in my mouth but I was able to keep it inside. I sat down in my chair and looked up at the sky. My head started spinning and I closed my eyes…big mistake. A strong feeling of nausea over took me and I ran towards the washroom. I threw up in the pot. My head was still spinning and I closed my eyes again. Another projectile vomit escaped my mouth. I flushed and removed my clothes and put them in the washing machine. I ran the shower and turned the lights of the wash room out. I put on some music on my phone and sat under the lukewarm water running from the shower naked…hoping that the feeling would pass away. It didn't pass…I passed out.

I got up the next day and found myself lying down naked, shivering on the bathroom floor. The shower was still running even though the water was warm I was feeling cold. I dressed up and checked my temperature. I was running a high fever. I had even caught a cold. It reminded me of the day when I had fainted like this on New Year's. My condition deteriorated over the next couple of months.

January – April 2011

I had spent another New Year's all by myself. My drinking did not stop. I was consuming more and more alcohol as the days passed by. I was even smoking a lot…I finished a pack a day. The blackouts had become a common occurrence and they stopped bothering me. Some days I would find myself lying in the kitchen or on the terrace or in the washroom in my own vomit. There were very few days when I would wake up to find myself sleeping peacefully on my bed. I think my brain function was deteriorating as well as I hardly seemed to remember anything from the previous night.

College had started once again and I was in third year. I did not go to college. I didn't see any point in going. My life was a mess and even though I did not give a shit…I didn't want anyone to see me this way. Even Preeti did not visit me very often now. Once in a blue moon she would show up to check out how I was. She tried to have a talk with me about the way I was living my life but I waved off all such talks. I knew she cared for me and meant well but I even knew for a fact that she was falling in love with me. I did not see myself in a place to enter in a relationship and always kept her at an arm's length…thinking that she would come out of it.

I think the worst time started somewhere in February when I started seeing things. I mean as in hallucinating. I started seeing random bright lights which blurred my vision in the beginning. Then they were followed by obscure figures. One night it finally happened when I saw real people…and heard them talk to me.

I had just finished drinking four beers and was lying on my bed when I saw her walk out through my wall. It was Aarti and she was standing right in front of me. She was wearing a white short *kurti* and black jeans. Her eyes were watery and like a puppy just as I remembered. She felt so real.

'What is wrong with you Aman.' She spoke.

I did not know whether I was to respond or not.

'Why are you doing this to yourself…There is a whole world in front of you which is left for you to be conquered…why are you throwing your life away. Why are you hurting the people who care for you…why are you being so selfish…why Aman why…tell me' her words seemed to echo around the room.

'Ya tell me Aman.' Came another voice from the other side. I saw Riya standing by the door dressed similarly as Aarti. 'Why did you do this Aman…why?…I loved you so much Aman why did you let me go? You hurt me Aman…I loved you so much and you hurt me. You hurt me Aman…you hurt me.' The room was echoing with their words.

'I am sorry…I am so very sorry…please forgive me…I am sorry.' I said as I closed my eyes and put my hands on my ears hoping that they would go away. But they didn't. The voices were echoing in my head now. And when I opened my eyes they were still there.

'Remember Aman…I told you I will kill you if you leave me…I am here to kill you. I am here to kill Aman…I am going to kill you.' Riya said and let out an evil laughter.

'Don't' please don't…leave me alone…leave me alone.' I said getting all paranoid.

'Come to me sweetheart…I will save you…hurry…run or she will kill you…come.' Aarti said and opened her arms for me.

I got off my bed and went dashing towards Aarti looking at Riya as she chased me with a dagger. I felt my head bang against the wall as I collapsed on the floor and passed out.

That wasn't the last I saw of them…they became a common occurrence in what I had realized were just hallucinations. But sometimes things seemed so real that it got very difficult to differentiate if a thing was real or if I was hallucinating.

One evening I almost bashed up my car on the footpath because I saw a road divider which wasn't even there. I was definitely losing it. I had become a threat to the society and to myself and so I decided to stay within the confined space of my house.

May 2011

It was just another night when I had been drinking. I was at the peak of my self-destruction when I had an insight. And somehow I knew that this insight would change my life and put me back on my feet.

Emptiness…that's what I felt tonight. There was something about this night that got me all pensive. I don't know what it was…maybe it was the weather…or maybe it was the song I had been listening to since the morning…it might have been those heavy medical books lying untouched in front of me… but whatever it was I was feeling Empty.

Today I didn't wanna feel love…I didn't wanna feel that something was missing…neither was I pinning on having that one person by my side. I didn't wanna step out and be with friends and family...I just wanted to sit alone in my room and wanted to let this feeling of emptiness enroll me. I wanted to drown myself in this sloth and feel free to think or question what I wanted to...I wanted to feel free to dream...I wanted to feel free and be peaceful.

It had been quite some time since I had felt peaceful. There had been too much of work...too much of running around...complicated thoughts...unanswered questions...fear...and above all... that irritating nag...that why did life have to be this way? Why couldn't it be less complicated? Why didn't all those dreams I had built as a kid ever come true.

I don't know why...but today it dawned on me...that if we weren't made to go through pain...or struggle...we would never know the value of anything. I did not realize how much something meant to me until I lost it.

Loss...it sounds like a very painful word. A lost friendship...a lost connection...a lost feeling...lost love. The weird thing is that no matter how painful it is...no matter how much you suffer...this feeling of being lost is addictive. You always get some kind of pleasure out of it...you drown into it. It makes you think about and analyze all those things ...those worries... that you had locked somewhere within you...and left the key to your destiny. And when destiny had finally unlocked it...it had made you lose that one thing you feared losing the most.

Fear...I had always thought of fear as being love's constant companion. I will not call it love's best friend...because it surely does not add any joy to it...but fear is something which always tags along uninvited when you start to love someone. The fear of losing that person…the fear that person will not love you back…fear that they will stop loving you…fear that this happiness, those few moments which feel surreal will come to an end one day. We as people try all sorts of permutations and combinations to suppress this fear. We think that we make our own life. We decide how we want it to be. We guide ourselves. But the truth is…we don't decide anything. We always leave the key to our destiny. All we have to ourselves at the end of everything are memories… questions…realizations. Some concerned faces asking us to move on and get on with our life. A practical and matured mind signaling us to believe… 'Maybe that it wasn't meant to be.' A wounded heart crying out loud… 'Maybe it was love.' And a soul which is filled with vast Emptiness.

My head felt a lot clearer. I didn't seem to need the alcohol anymore. I guess I was finally ready to accept the reality and pick up whatever pieces of my life I could find and put them back together. I was ready to take life as it came to me. There were no more hallucinations…no more voices asking me to kill myself. Just a strong head waiting for all of this to end.

21

FRIENDS WITH BENEFITS...ARE YOU RETARDED?

Summer 2011

The summer was at its peak. The mercury had risen to a scorching 48 degrees. I was back in Nagpur and it felt as if I was reliving the same old summer days when Aarti had left me three years ago. The loneliness ... The long jobless days and the short sleepless nights...everything just seemed the way it was three years ago.

Preeti was in Nagpur too for her summer internship at Raymond's. She called me a lot of times...asking me to come and meet her. She wanted me to take her out and show her around the city...my city. I wasn't keeping well these days and had been running a fever. I didn't eat much and had lost my appetite. I had been feeling awfully weak and thus I preferred to stay indoors.

It was finally the day when Preeti's internship got over. She was flying back to Mumbai the next day. She called me around 12.30 PM and asked me if I could meet her for a cup of coffee somewhere.

Although I really did not have the strength to even move a muscle…I thought that it would be very rude on my part to wave this off. I hadn't met her even once during her stay in Nagpur and I guess this coffee date was the least I could have done. I agreed to meet her at the CCD in Law College square at four – four thirty.

'So what's up?' Preeti said after we placed our order and took our seats in CCD.

'Nothing much…you tell me.' I said.

'How have you been?' she asked

'Fantastic.' I said sarcastically.

'What is wrong with you…you seem to have lost a lot of weight.' She said.

'Ya I have been dieting.' I said with sarcasm dripping from each word.

'Aman…be serious for once…Are you alright? You look so…blue.' She said getting all concerned.

'Well if you must know…I am not alright. I am running a high fever and I can't even move properly.' I said getting a little irritated.

'Why what happened… did you see a doctor?' she asked. Her words were now just adding fuel to my irritation.

'My entire family is full of doctors…obviously I have seen a doctor Preeti.' I said.

'And what did they say?' gosh …I thought to myself…will her questions never end.

'Look Preeti…I am alright…and I am not here to discuss my health problems with you okay.' I told her quite frankly.

'Okay fine…' she said and paused for a few seconds. 'Nagpur is a nice place *yaar.*' She continued.

'Yup.' I said as I got down to sipping my coffee.

'It would have been nice if you took me out somewhere *yaar.* I missed you so much during my stay here. And you always kept giving me some or the other excuse for not meeting.' She said all dreamily.

'Hey…they weren't excuses. Look at me…I'm sick…you want me to come and party with you like this?' I told her.

'Why are you being so obnoxious Aman…it's not that I'm blaming you or anything.' She said. I could see that she was getting a little irritated herself.

'Preeti…I have not come here to listen to this bullshit again. If you have anything important to say…then please tell me quickly. I am not feeling well.' I said calmly.

'Hey I'm not forcing you to stay…you can go if you want to. And *waise bhi* there is not much left to say…if you can't understand me…then there is no point in saying it.' she said and looked the other way.

'You think I don't understand you…well I know exactly what you want to say. You want to tell me that over the time you have known me…you have started liking me. You think I am fun to be with and you might think you are even in love me or some other sentimental stuff like that. Isn't that right? And I have known this ever since the day you asked me to move in with you. It doesn't take a genius to figure it out.' It felt like I had just performed a by-pass surgery on her heart… and had picked the words and the feelings out of it and had laid them out on the table.

'If you knew what I was feeling all this while… then why didn't you say something? Why didn't you show that you felt the same way Aman? Why?' she said. Her eyes were looking at me as if they were searching for the answers to all those questions she had.

'Because I don't feel the same way about you.' I said. 'I don't love you.'

'Oh…' a long pause followed before she continued. 'So in this past year since we have known each other…have you never had any feelings for me? All those moments which we spent together…didn't they mean anything to you? Because they meant a lot to me…I really thought that maybe someday we will get together and things wouldn't be just about the sex.' her voice got softer with every word she said. It seemed as if she was searching for the dimmest ray of hope which would have saved her the heart break.

'Feelings are overrated Preeti…all they leave you with is a lot of pain. I think we were better off the way we started. Friends with benefits…that is where we should have left things.' I said.

She remained quiet for some time and after taking a large sip of her coffee she said… 'If that is how you feel Aman…then I guess there is nothing else left to say.'

'Preeti…' I wanted to give her one of my philosophical lectures about how tough life is and how you are supposed to live with it…but she cut me short.

'Aman please…I don't want your sympathy. If you have anything else to tell me then you can say it…or else I think you should go.' She looked at me…she was still searching for something…anything…hope, love or just a shoulder to cry on that I could provide her with. 'Is there anything left for you to say?' she asked again.

'I guess not.' I said.

'Bye Aman.' She said as she got up, picked up her bag and left the coffee shop.

'Bye.' I said to her disappearing figure.

I cleared the bill and got out into Law College Square. It was five thirty in the evening and the sun was still shining brightly. There was a lot of hustle in the square as people were making their way home from work. A group of students in their college uniforms had gathered outside Archie's Gallery. Young couples were making their way into CCD for their dates. I suddenly realized that I did not fit into this whole atmosphere of the youthful hustle bustle anymore. I got inside my car and started driving.

22
WHERE IT ALL ENDS...

July 2011

I started driving on Amaravati Road. The memories of the way I and Preeti had parted were still fresh in my head. I felt sad that things had to end this way between us. But that is what the scenario had been in the last one year or so. Nothing seemed to have a happy ending.

If only I could have told her the truth. It was not just her...I had lied to Riya...lied to Krish, Madhur and Aisha...I had lied to myself. Somewhere within me I had told myself that everything was going to be okay. That was a big fat lie. The truth was horrifying. Every time I thought about it...it sent a chill down my spine. Every time I looked back at that day...I shivered with fear. The memories of that night when I had fainted on New Year's 2010 flashed me by and a tear rolled down my eye as I continued to drive.

I had woken up to find myself lying down on a bed in what seemed like a room in the D –Wing of Dr.D.Y.Patil Hospital. Dr.Anubhav who was a Medicine Resident in the hospital was standing next to me. He was removing the I.V drip I had been on. I did not know how I had reached here. The last thing I remembered was feeling dizzy standing in front of my college and fainting.

'Hey champ…how do you feel?' Anubhav asked.

'I feel alright… I guess.' I said as I rubbed my eyes to get a better picture of my surroundings. 'Where are my specs?' I asked.

Anubhav picked them up from the table opposite my bed and handed them to me. 'Here you go.' He said.

'What happened to me? How did I get here?' I asked him.

'Well…you fainted last night in front of the college. The guards brought you to the casualty. We suspected it was due to the excessive drinking…but…' he paused.

'But… what?' I asked him.

'The alcohol content in your blood wasn't significant for an episode like that so we admitted you for overnight monitoring.' he said.

'And…did you find anything?' he was making me nervous.

'Chill dude…you are going to be alright.' I sensed hesitation in his voice. I wasn't convinced.

'What was the I.V for?' I asked

'Nothing… it is just your regular immunosuppressant which you have been prescribed. Don't worry…everything is fine. Now take your time and when you feel alright come downstairs…Dr.Sinha wants to have a word with you.' He said and left my room.

Dr.Sinha was the senior most M.D Medicine doctor in the hospital.

I felt a little relieved…if he was on my case then I was in good hands. I got off my bed and freshened up in the washroom. I changed out of my hospital gown and walked downstairs to Dr. Sinha's cabin. The receptionist summoned me in.

'Come Aman *beta* take a seat.' He said.

I sat down in the chair in front of his desk. 'Good morning sir.' I said.

'So tell me…how do you feel?' He asked me.

'I feel alright sir.' I said.

'It looks like someone has been drinking a lot.' He said and smiled.

'Well you know sir…it was New Year's…and I only had a couple of beers.' I said shyly…he was my professor after all.

'Oh ya I know…good old college days.' He said.

'So what happened to me sir? Did I faint because of the drinks?' I asked him.

'Where do you stay Aman?' He asked. His voice got a little serious now.

'I stay in the hostel sir. Why are you asking?' I said.

'No which city do you stay in?' he asked again ignoring my questions.

'I am from Nagpur sir.' I said. He looked down at the file on his table and puffed his cheeks. 'What's the matter sir?' I asked him.

'Can your parents fly in today by any chance?' He asked.

'What is the problem sir? Please tell me…you are making me very nervous.' I said.

'Aman…it is better to talk about it with your parents around.' He said.

'Sir…please tell me…I am a major now…I can deal with it.' I said.

'Ok fine then Aman…listen very carefully.' He said and I leaned in towards him to show that I was all ears. 'Aman…you know that you have Porphyria right.' He said.

'Yes sir… it is a congenital disease…I have it since childhood.' I said.

'Yes…you are right. This disease manifests itself in different ways as you grow up. You never know when it can get serious. With adequate medication it can be controlled.' He said.

'Yes sir…I have been taking my medicines according to the prescription. I have been taking all those immunosuppressants since I was a kid.' I said.

'I know that Aman…but in your case the disease has turned out to be a very rare manifestation of it.' He said.

'And what is that?' I asked as my heart started pounding like it had never before.

'Sometime the disease worsens as a side effect of the medication and starts progressing faster.' He said.

'So now what has to be done?' I asked hoping that he had some good news for me.

'I am afraid that there is nothing that can be done once the disease reaches this point.' He said.

'So does that mean I am going to…die?' I asked…the last word came out more like a murmur.

'I am sorry.' He said and rubbed his palm over my shoulder. I was shocked… devastated. A sinking feeling over took me. A lot of thoughts started a stampede in my head. I looked around to see if this was a trick. I wanted Cyrus Brocha to jump out from somewhere and tell me that I was the *Bakra*. There was no one in there… no hidden cameras…nothing. I was at a loss of words.

'How much time?' I asked him.

'I don't know…maybe a year…maybe ten…that doesn't matter…I think you should be with loved ones…' he continued with his sympathetic doctor speech and told me that the fainting episodes would get more common etc etc. I only heard half of what he was saying. I felt numb and my mind was running all over the place.

It was a joke! Yeah that's what it was…God was joking with me! Life was bullying me. It is funny how we use words like KILL and DEAD a zillion times in a day.

"I will kill you if you don't reach here in another ten minutes…"Aisha had said a few days back when I had gotten late at picking her up from her hostel as I had overslept.

"AMAN…you ass….if you screw up this game anymore…soon you'll be dead meat!" Krish had said rather angrily over a DOTA game as I kept losing my co-ordination because of Riya's constant buzzing of "I love u" messages.

And then Riya. "I love you sweetheart. I love you so very much…and I am going to continue doing that for the rest of my life…till DEATH did us apart"…this was something we told each other every day…at the end of every conversation…as we retired into the night with dreams of spending our entire life together. With each night….with each conversation…..the dreams just kept getting bigger. I knew that it was just the beginning of our relationship….and we were not at the right age of deciding and planning anything…but that didn't stop us from dreaming!

It's crazy how each time you fall in love, you feel this is it. This is just what you were searching for. There were times I would picture two oldies…holding each other's hand…cribbing to each other about their knee problems…fighting with each other for not taking their daily medicines at time…but at the end of it…still loving each other. And in them I would picture the two of us. I had fallen in love with Riya in the last one year….now all I wished for was to grow in love with her. But each time you think you have found the love of your life…the world just had to come crashing down on you.

There is always that one day when Fate pays you a random visit and tells you softly… "Dude….dump all your dreams into a waste basket! You don't decide anything…I will take you where you really need to be."

Today was that day. A New Year had begun for me…just to make me realize that maybe I won't be ALIVE to witness the next New Year's. I was going to be DEAD! Dead….the word itself send a shiver down my spine. My head felt tizzy…my fingers were going numb…I couldn't feel my limbs anymore…my knees were too weak to hold me. I found the first seat next to the elevator and crashed on it. I stared blankly at the file in my hand. PORPHYRIA…the disease that I never regarded any significance in my life was now killing me.

I turned to face a middle aged lady with her unwell five year old. The lady kept wiping the kid's dripping nose with a handkerchief. Her face filled with concern….her eyes filled with love…immense motherly love. Her husband entered the picture with a packet of medicines in his hand. "Awley mera raja beta…" said the lady as she lifted that kid in her arms and almost immediately her husband planted a peck on the kid's forehead.

I watched those strange figures disappear into the corridor's end and suddenly I felt even more depressed.

I could picture mom running behind me with a bottle of syrup in her hand. "Aman…*beta one spoon…please mumma ke liye!*"… "Nooo…mom not that yucky syrup again…I don't like it!" I said in my kiddish accent with my hands folded and puffed cheeks. And then from nowhere dad crept in slowly from behind, cradled his hand around my waist and lifted me in one wisp of a second. He was hiding something behind his back. He told me he would give it to me only if I drank that disgusting syrup. I had no choice left…I gulped it down my throat as fast as I could. The next thing I saw was a huge toy jet plane emerging from his other hand. My happiness knew no bounds…I was overjoyed. I hugged my dad almost immediately and declared out loud, "I love you dad!"…to which he reciprocated by saying "we love you too son" He hugged me back as tightly as he could…mom cuddled around us from behind.

The thought itself made me crave for a hug…I wanted mom and dad to come right away and hug me the same way…and tell me what had happened was just a bad dream. I wanted them to come and tell me that I was going to be fine…I am not dying!

'*Bhaisabh….thoda jaga do na….mere bete ko baithna hai*' said an old wrinkled faced man as he pointed out his handicapped son to me. I immediately gathered my thoughts and got to my feet making place for that boy. I left the hospital…and kept walking. I walked and I walked until I realized I didn't know where I was heading. I didn't take the elevator up to the sixth floor. I chose to climb. The crude reality hadn't sunk in yet. I didn't know when was I going to die…what was coming up for me…what all would I go through before I was finally declared dead…but right now what I felt was DEAD! I had died already!

After climbing about nine floors I finally made it to my hostel room. My throat was parched but I didn't feel like drinking water. My stomach was churning as I hadn't eaten anything…but I didn't feel like eating either. My head was heavy…burdened with a cascade of memories…but still it felt blank. YES….I was already feeling it. I was feeling DEAD!

I was in a state of shock and everything just seemed unreal. I wanted someone to pour a bucket of water on me and wake me up from this horrid nightmare. I stared at nothing with my eyes wide open for hours together before my eyelids finally gave up and closed them shut.

I woke up late in the evening and found my file still lying down next to my bed. I hadn't been dreaming. All of it was true…all of this was fucking true. I checked my phone for the first time after that night. It had 22 missed calls from Riya…and 5 from home. There were a few unread messages in my inbox…most of them from Riya. "Why aren't you picking up your damn phone???…call me asap" was the content of half of them. I scrolled down to the first message I had received from her. "Happy anniversary sweetheart…I love you a lot. I always have. Don't ever leave me…..it would actually kill me. Loads of hugs and kisses."

I ran to my bathroom…and stood below the shower with my clothes on. I cried like a mad man. I had to leave behind everyone whom I loved…and who loved me. It was the thought of my loved one's crying over my dead body that made me fear death! I had always felt that the older you grow…the lesser are the number of people weeping for you. There are those many faces who weep a little and move on with their life…there are those many more who don't show any signs of grief…and then again there are those faces that disappear altogether. But at the end of it there are those few people who you know…who love you more than anything in this world…these are the few hearts you know you would live in even after you are long gone and buried. Seeing them in pain…suffering…because of you…is something that makes you fear death indeed. It was the toughest thing I had to do. It was time to get on with it. I finally took my cell phone and scrolled down my contact list. I called DAD.

"Hi Dad"I said.

"Hi son…how are you? How is everything back there?" he said.

"Dad what are you doing? Are you busy with something?" I enquired.

"No…was just finishing off for the day. God, it was a long tiring day…five surgeries back to back. I feel pretty exhausted." he said as he led out a sigh.

"Uhh okay...do you want me to call back later?" I checked sensing the exhaustion in his voice.

"*Arre no beta.* You tell me...how come you called this late?" he asked, now concerned.

"Dad I want to come home.....I want to see you people." I said, my voice cracking up.

"Aman, are you fine son? What is bothering you?" he asked this time worried.

"No dad I just want to come home. Please..." I said almost pleading.

"Okay...I will book your ticket right away. Take the first flight back home tomorrow...and remember we love you" he said, assuring me.

"I love you too dad" I said as I hung up on him and burst into tears.

Any kind of love was killing me right now. But I had one more task left. I had to call Riya. Or even message her for that matter. I took the easy way and decided to message her.

"Hey Riya. Sorry babes, couldn't take your calls or reply to any of your messages. Got totally sloshed on New Year's and was knocked out for 24 hours straight. Then I woke up and went back to sleep again. Have been pretty dazed lately. So yeah, anyway...I will be going to Alibaugh with the guys. It is Shreenivas's birthday. Will be out for another day. So won't be able to call you. Your's Aman."

I sent her the message at 3.30 in the night. I was pretty sure by the time she got it I would be home. But did I want to tell her that I was coming back? Did I want her to know about what had happened to me? I guess no. That's why I lied. I lied to the girl I loved the most. I lied because I couldn't see her shatter into pieces in front of me. I couldn't see her in the same pain I had gone through when Aarti died. I just couldn't. So I lied.

Nagpur. I was back. Back home. Back to that city where the three people I loved the most were. Every place in this city bought back a cascade of memories. As I walked towards the exit sign on the airport gate, I saw dad standing there waiting for me. He never came otherwise. He would always send the driver. But today he was here. I think he had sensed it. He had sensed that something was terribly wrong just by hearing my voice. I walked towards him and he welcomed me with a warm hug. I hugged him as tightly as I could have. Generally such things embarrass me in public. But today….nothing mattered. I was home, finally.

Dad drove me home. We hardly spoke during the entire journey. We reached home…Mom hadn't gone to her clinic yet. She was waiting for the two of us to arrive equally concerned. She hurriedly opened the door as I rang the doorbell.

"Aman. …" she spoke in her motherly voice as she cuddled my face with her hands and planted a kiss on my forehead and then hugged me. They both sat in front of me with questions in their eyes at the dining table for minutes together. This was the part I was dreading the most. I wanted to spill it out…tell them everything and face the reality. Face it for once and get over with it…but all I managed was "Mom…and dad…I am tired. I want to sleep."

"Yeah…sure sweetheart. Anything you wish to do." They said and made it easier for me.

I retired into my bed for the rest of the day. The only time I came out was to have dinner. Mom had made my favorite chicken. There was nothing better than the feeling of being at home with your loved ones and mom's home cooked food. Even though they were both really worried as to what had happened to me…they had decided to keep quiet and give me my space and time. It's just the connection I feel…your parents are the only two people who can sense each and every thought in your mind and empathize with it.

It was late in the evening. Mom and Dad had just come back home after a long day's work. Mom finished her evening prayers and dad took a quick shower and seated himself on the sofa with the news channel on. As both of them settled down after slogging for hours in the hospital…I finally gathered the courage and stepped out of my room into the living room.

"Mom…dad I need to talk to you" I declared in a little higher than usual tone. Dad immediately switched of the TV and mom rushed out of kitchen as fast as she could. They both sat on the sofa facing me. There was a huge pause.

"What is bothering you son?" mom asked finally.

"Mom…dad…I fainted on the New Year's Eve. Was admitted in hospital for two days." I said as I saw their facial expressions change.

"WHAT??? You were in the hospital for two days and we had no clue? " dad said rather seriously.

"I met Dr. Sinha, the head of the Medicine department." I said ignoring their questions. "And he called me in and told me that my porphyria had worsened. He says the medicines I have been taking all these years have worsened it… And he is afraid that now it is…" I stopped there. I felt like I was chocking.

"Aman, say…now what?" mom said, with a scared expression on her face.

"He says it is now untreatable…he says I don't have much time in my hands. He thinks….I'm going to die." I felt numb as I finally disclosed the news of my death to my parents.

Tears rolled down mom's shocked eyes. Dad dropped the remote in his hand. They sat there silently for several minutes…trying to cope up with the reality which still hadn't sunk in for me.

"I think there must be something wrong. Who the hell is Dr. Sinha? We are going to take a second opinion. We will show you to the best medicine practitioner. I am sure something must have been wrong. This isn't possible…this is just not true" Mom said in a rather panicky tone convincing herself with a lie. She looked devastated. She didn't know what she was going to do. It looked as if she wanted to fight with god, with destiny and undo this thing altogether. She ran around the entire house looking for the phone diary so that she could call up someone…anyone who could tell her that her son was going to be fine. She went to every corner in the living room…desperately searching for a ray of hope and then returned back to my dad who hadn't moved an inch yet. He looked shocked…it looked like someone had sucked the life out of him. My mom pulled his t-shirt pleading him to do something…to say something. I sat there watching the two people who had dreamed and prayed for their son's happiness shatter into pieces. I sat there and cried my heart out....watching them in pain.

"Mom, they ran the tests three times. There have been no mistakes. I am going to DIE.Mom I am going to die…"I said weeping heavily.

"No…don't…don't cry.…..it's all going to be fine. We will figure out a way together…"she cried harder as she convinced herself more than me.

Finally dad broke his silence and tears rolled down his cheek. He cried….with his hands on his face. All three of us sitting there knew it was all true. Watching dad cry is something I could never bare…it always ran a chill down my spine. That day I had seen that old helpless man sitting there…who had no way he could save his only son. I had sensed his misery…being the best surgeon in town he didn't know a way to save his own son's life. I had seen the strongest man I knew shatter into pieces. They both cuddled me into their arms and three of us cried our heart out. That night I slept with my parents and after ages I had slept so peacefully.

It was a new day…but there was no sunshine. Reality had smacked us all in our faces. Mom and dad sat alone for hours together in silence. The days would just pass by…and even with three people and a dog in the house…it felt deserted. After two days of constant silence and watching my parents die each day from within I finally decided to go and talk to dad.

"Dad I think I should go back." I said.

"Are you out of your mind? You are going nowhere. You are staying with us." He replied rather seriously.

"No dad. I need to go back. I can't see you people this way. There are a lot of things I need to sort out and I need my own time…my own space." I said making my point clear.

"Why are you doing this? I will take you to Europe. You can go sky- diving as you always wanted to…" he said breaking down.

"No dad I need to get back. Please allow me." I said requesting him to live the last few days of my life by myself.

I guess my parents had nothing much left to say. They agreed to everything I asked them for. They had been the best parents one could ever have. Even though it killed to let me go…they did. The next evening I took a flight and I was back in Mumbai.

As all those memories ran in my head…I realized why I had hidden the truth froms everyone who cared for me. It was painful…after listening to my parents break down like that I did not want anyone else to feel such pain again. I did not want anyone to feel sad because of me.

'It is better to let go of someone who loves you…than keeping him… in love with you, when you know you just can't be with him' were the last words Aarti had said to me. They made a lot of sense now. Those words had defined me and my actions in the last one and a half years. I broke up with Riya because I did not want her to feel the same pain that I felt when Aarti had died. I fought with Krish, Madhur and Aisha because I knew they cared for me too much and my death would have left them devastated. As for Preeti…I needed someone by my side when the entire world deserted me. I hoped every day that I spent with her that she wouldn't fall for me. But I think that is the way of life...everything that you hope for never happens.

As I drove on the wide highway my vision started blurring and memories from my past flashed me by. I saw myself as a little child playing on the swings and the slides in my school. My school had been such a vital component of my life growing up. I remembered all my favorite teachers who used to keep nagging me to improve my handwriting. I saw myself and my friends playing soccer in the lunch break on the school playground. It had been such a long time since I had talked to them. Ever since I had entered college I had lost all contact with them. I wanted to call them and ask them how they were doing. I wanted to kick a football... something that I hadn't done ever since I left school.

I remembered the times when I shared lunch with Aarti...my first love. I remembered how while growing up we used to steal glances at each-other in between classes. All those long phone conversations played themselves in my head. I saw all those evenings we spent together in the swimming pool. I used to cut the schedule my coach gave me short so that I could have a chat with her. I remembered how happy she was when I won my first gold medal. That record holding nine hour long conversation on the day I asked her out...it all seemed so fresh in my head. I could never forget her eyes and the way they looked at me when we had kissed for the first time. The thought of her untimely death and her last words still haunted me.

As one chapter of my life came to an end...another unfolded. Riya...the girl who loved me more than I could have imagined. If it wasn't for her…I would have never found out how beautiful the world was. All those long drives and those evening walks…I longed for them. That beautiful winter evening and that candlelight supper when I had asked her out…it still brought back the feeling of joy. The afternoon that we spent together making love still made me believe that we were perfect for each other. All those long distance phone calls we had shared whispering soft nothings to each-other…now only brought tears to my eyes. I wanted to call her and tell her what an ass I had been. 'Try not to hate me Riya…try not to hate Me.' is what I wanted to tell her. I guess it was the selfish side of me that was urging me to gather some sympathy out of whatever life of mine remained. But now that the damage was done…there was no point crying over it.

I remembered the enthusiasm with which I had landed in Mumbai and that first day of college. I thought about Aisha and how she had been a complete sweetheart to me. I remembered how Krish and Madhur had become an integral part of my life and how our friendship had blossomed over time. All those memories of Goa were reeling right in front of me and I remembered how the three of us were carefree and happy. That day on the Margoa station when Krish had told me that he loved me…little did I know that those days were never coming back. Even as all those memories of the crazy ass fun we had together managed to bring a smile on my face…the flashes of that night when we had parted ways filled my heart with sorrow.

My legs grew weak and I could no longer keep them on the accelerator. I stopped my car and got outside to get some fresh air. It was around six in the evening and an orangish sun was still shining on the horizon. I had been driving in a daze and had no idea where I was standing. After walking for a few minutes I found myself outside the Ambazari Garden. I knew this place. I walked for a few minutes more and soon I was standing on that cliff overlooking the lake. My legs couldn't hold me any longer and I decided to sit down.

I saw a group of guys standing with their bikes, smoking a few meters away from where I was sitting. They laughed and patted each other...they looked totally engrossed in their conversation. They seemed happy...carefree. I smiled as I saw a shadow of Krish Madhur and myself in them. 'Innocent buggers' I thought to myself. They didn't have the slightest idea how harsh life could get on them. Then again I stared into infinity. I stared into the infinite depth of that lake which was in front of me. I saw nothing but a reflection of myself. I saw a reflection of me sitting on a cliff all alone looking down at no one but myself. I heard voices...voices that seemed to originate from somewhere deep down inside that lake. They sounded as if someone was talking through a long hollow pipe. I tried to look deeper trying to find out the source of those voices. I found nothing. I thought maybe they were just in my head and tried paying attention to them. I closed my eyes and I recognized them. They were those laughs and giggles we had shared together. They were those slangs we hurled at each-other on daily basis. I opened my eyes with a start and felt tears creep up in them. I had an urge to call Krish... but soon overcame it and tossed my cell phone into the lake. Now I knew one thing for sure. I was not going to Goa with the guys ever again.

I wanted to feel love in my life. Not just the artful postures of love…but love that overthrows life. Un-biddable, Ungovernable love like a riot in the heart…and nothing to be done could ruin or rapture. Jon Bon Jovi had said that 'No Man is an island'. But I guess I had proved him wrong. I had lived my life in the past one year all by myself…yet I still felt that something was missing. I thought maybe all this had been a mistake after all.

This was the place where Aarti had left me three years ago. This was the cliff where it had all begun. I looked at the lake in front of me. The water had the same greenish tint to it. I wondered how my life had changed so drastically in the past three years. Did I have any regrets…maybe a few. A dream left unfulfilled. A few words left unsaid. A relationship which never ran its due course. A friendship left in shambles. An untimely death. Was all this worth the pain?

Today as I sat on this cliff with the summer of my life at its peak…I didn't need the answers of those million questions my heart asked me. I didn't need anyone to tell me that it was all going to be okay. I did not want a breeze of happiness to blow through my life. All I needed was the peace. All I needed was the rain. Life had taken a full circle and had brought me back to the same place…all by myself… lonely and lost.

My life was coming to an end. I looked up at the sky and saw the school of birds flying home…the sun was setting in the horizon…relieving the world from its heat. My head felt heavy and my body felt weak…my vision was blurring and a feeling of dizziness enrolled me. I closed my eyes and allowed my body to lay down flat on that cliff.

I knew that these were the last few breaths I would ever take. And

I spread my hands apart in my last prayer. I prayed to God that if he ever gave me another life… let me be born to the same parents…let me have Krish as a friend…let me have Aarti as my love…let Riya be as wonderful as she is and let me have those happy rains. I felt a cool breeze blowing, which made me open my eyes for the last time. Above me I saw grey clouds covering the dimly lit sky. I saw the leaves of the trees moving. I heard the birds chirping as I felt a drop of water strike my forehead. The weather changed and I found myself fighting for breath. AND THEN IT RAINED…and everything seemed beautiful again.

EPILOGUE

July 2011

It was rather cold for a July morning in Nagpur. It had been raining heavily. The street outside the old VCA Cricket Stadium was busy as cars zoomed in to enter the church premises opposite it. A lot of people wearing different shades of black and grey could be seen entering the church.

Inside the church a lot of familiar faces were seen sitting on the benches right in front of the altar. Aman's Dad and Mom were sitting in the first row. A lot of his relatives had come. Krish, Madhur and Aisha had flown in from Delhi to witness something that nobody wanted to believe. Riya sat in the second row behind Aman's Mom and her sorrow seemed to have crossed all boundaries. She cried and cried and cried. A lot of Aman's classmates from school and college had also come to offer their condolences. No one present inside that church wanted to believe that Aman…that happy bugger…was no more. But that body in the coffin, lying peacefully next to the altar suggested differently.

The priest came up to the altar.

'Good morning…and a warm welcome to you all on this cold day.' He spoke. 'Our service will begin in a few minutes…but first we have asked James…Aman's father to say a few words'

Aman's Dad got up from his seat and came up to the altar to give his speech. He stood there for some time and tried to compose himself. It all seemed very difficult. He had to talk about his own son's death to a gathering of people who were eagerly awaiting his words. A drop of tear rolled down his cheek. He wiped it off with his handkerchief and finally spoke.

'When Aman's grandfather expired he came up to me and told me that he preferred funerals to weddings. He said it was easier to get enthusiastic about a ceremony he had an outside chance of being involved in. ' he said. And the gathering let out a subdued laugh. He continued.

'In order to prepare this speech I rang a few people to get a general picture of how Aman was regarded by the people who had met him. I think that was the way many of you found out that he was no more. Funny…seems to have been a word people most connected with him. Terribly sarcastic also rang a lot of bells. So very funny and very sarcastic seems to have been the strangest view point. On the other hand some of you have been kind enough to ring me up and let me know that you loved him…which I know he would have been thrilled to hear. You remember his fabulous hospitality… his strange experimental cooking. The recipe of his Dashing Chicken fortunately goes with him to his grave. Most of all you tell me about his enormous capacity for joy and when joyful…of highly vocal drunkenness. But I hope joyful is how you will remember him. For me he was my son… my son whom I was very proud of. He was what made living worthwhile. And today I am just sorry…I am sorry for all those uncountable times when I wanted to hug and tell him that I loved him and I didn't. I am sorry son. I love you and I always will.' His voice cracked up and the tears didn't seem to hold back as they came flooding in not only his eyes but in every eye that was present there.

'Aman once told me that it is better to let go of someone who loves you…than keeping him… in love with you, when you know you just can't be with him. But today when I look at all you people who have come out here to pay homage to him. I think maybe he was wrong. I think we are not the ones who choose who loves us after all. Now I would like to ask anyone present here to come up and say a few words about Aman if they please.' With this he went back and took his seat next to Aman's Mom who was way past the point of break down.

A lot of people came up to the altar and narrated stories about Aman and how he had an impact on their lives. Finally Krish got up from his seat and came to the altar.

'Hello… my name is Krish Tandon. I am Aman's batch mate from college. I guess that's all what was left between us. I always considered him to be my best friend…but the way that we parted ways was just horrifying. When Aman's Dad called me I thought it was a practical joke someone was playing on me. I had no idea what Aman was going through in the last days of his life as he alienated himself from not just me but everyone. I think he loved us a lot to see us get hurt when he was gone. But I think I would be doing injustice to friendship if I called myself his best friend. Never...not even once did I try to find out what was it that was bothering him. I am sorry Aman...I am so sorry.' Krish tried hard to fight his tears but they got the better of him and he broke down. After composing himself he continued

'As for me...you may ask how I would remember him...what I thought of him...unfortunately there I don't have words. Perhaps you will forgive me if I confer my feelings in the words of another splendid bugger... W.A.Jordan... this is actually what I want to say... Stop all the clocks...cut off the telephone...prevent the dog from barking with that juicy bone...silence the pianos and with muffled drums bring out the coffin...let the moaners come. The aero plane moaning overhead...scribbling on the sky the message...he is dead. He was my north...my south....my east and west...my work in week and my Sunday rest...my noon...my midnight...my talk...my song. I thought that love would last forever...I was wrong. The stars are not wanted now...pick out every one. Pack up the moon and dismantle the sun. Pour away the ocean and sweep out the woods...because nothing here can come to any good.'

THE AUTHOR SPEAKS

Hello everyone. This is Gaurav Dashputra and yes unfortunately I'm the author of this book. Writing this book was a tough job so I really hope everyone liked reading it. Here I want to tell you a little story about how I came about writing this book.

I was in 9th grade when I gave writing my first shot. I wrote a 30 page short story back then called Tokyo – Delhi Scheduled. It was a story of a guy who falls in love with a girl on a flight from Tokyo to Delhi which crashes in the Himalayas. Well that story never made its way out of a certain long book of mine which got lost in time. I had written that story for a certain someone whom I loved back then. And after she told me that it sucked crocodile balls…I thought writing wasn't my cup of tea.

Following a bad break up in 11th grade writing a novel first came in my head. I started writing a story inspired by my life. It was called Liar Liar Love's on Fire. I had written 5 chapters when a gang of guys threatened me to delete and abort it by holding a gun at my head (A little exaggeration) as I was defaming them. Unwillingly I had to give up writing back then.

As 12th grade came to an end and I had to decide a career path, I told my parents that I didn't want to become doctor. I said I would take up something like journalism to pursue writing. My parents back then thought I had gone nuts and took it upon themselves to make sure I made something out of my life. After 12th grade came to an end I came to Mumbai for college and had to end my long distance relationship with my high school sweetheart. That is what inspired me to give writing a second shot. I never finished writing my second untitled novel as I realized that the topic was just downright stupid.

In the summer of 2010 love struck me again and I was living a dream. But as you know that is the stark reality behind dreams...they leave you when you open your eyes. After just seeing each other for 3 – 4 months I and my girlfriend broke up in late September. It was around that time when I was lying down all alone on my bed at night looking into the empty darkness of my room and reaching to find some meaning in my hollow thoughts, I picturised a scene in my head. It was a man ailing for love. Over the next couple of the days as that scene never evaded my head and I started questioning as to who that man was. Working in the Medical field makes you come across a lot of suffering. Every day I saw people in pain, sick people, people dying and everyone who loved them, suffer with them.

But the worst kind of patients where the young kids and young adults who suffered from incurable congenital diseases. Every day I came across people like Aman who had so much to offer to the world but their disease had shattered them to a mere shadow of their being. I wondered day in and day out as to why was life so tough for them. What is it that they had done to receive such suffering from god? I questioned that whose fault was it anyway? The deeper I looked for the answers to these questions…the deeper I drowned into the scene of a man ailing for love. It was then that I started writing AND THEN IT RAINED…

When I started writing all I had seen was the upside of life. Everything seemed like a cake walk. But I knew writing this would be anything but that. In September 2011 I finished writing my book and it gave me an immense sense of satisfaction.

I was looking out for publishers when a lot of people close to me read the book. They were really cynical about it and told me that the story is really depressing and the Aman as a character has a very negative feeling about him. They wanted me to make it a little upbeat so that the story could have a good moral in it. Most of the Books and most of the movies I have read or seen in the life always end with a happy ending. Everyone tells me happy ending is what sells. But after seeing all the pain and suffering in the lives of my patients I beg to differ. I think reality is far beyond happy endings all the time. I think there are some issues that have to be dealt on a real level rather than just hiding the pain behind the cozy love stories we love so much.

Modern medicine is making progress every day and we have come a step closer to curing even those diseases which were a menace back in the days. When we were small kids all the stories we read came with a moral. That was how we knew things like "Tit For Tat" "A Friend in Need is A Friend Indeed" etc etc. With this book I want to take you all back in that time. I want to end this book with a message of my own. And that message is Genetic Counselling. Yes…Genetic Counselling is the only way by which all the Congenital Diseases can be controlled. It sure looks like a farfetched thought but it is the only way we can have a society free from diseases like Porphyria. It is the only way we can always have our happy endings. After all nothing in life that is worthwhile…comes easy.

Thank you for reading the book and I hope you liked it.